LEE WARREN

Mercy Inn: A Christmas Novella

The Mercy Inn Series (Book 1)

Do not neglect to show hospitality to strangers, for thereby some have entertained angels unawares.
(Hebrews 13:2)

For he will command his angels concerning you to guard you in all your ways.
(Psalm 91:11)

Are [the angels] not all ministering spirits sent out to serve for the sake of those who are to inherit salvation?
(Hebrews 1:14)

Chapter 1

"I just went through some town called Fox Creek on Highway 17," Megan Cahill said into her cell phone. "Can't wait to see what's next. You said this stretch of road would take my breath away, right?"

"You'll be heading into the San Juan Mountains soon," Rebecca said. "Wait 'til you see the Conejos River. It's so peaceful. And as you start to climb in elevation, you'll see cabins tucked between the mountains. You won't even see any roads leading to the cabins."

"Sounds wonderful," Megan said. "Think I'm going to beat the snow? I should be at your place in less than an hour."

"I've been watching the radar and the snow is getting close. Why don't you just get a room for the evening? The roads should be clear by tomorrow morning."

Snow had been falling for a while already, but Megan wasn't going to tell Rebecca that. "I'll be fine, mother." Megan always kidded her best friend from high school about how motherly she could be, but she was thankful for it during times like this. She had been racing the snow all day, but forecasters were only calling for three or four inches in southern Colorado. No big deal.

"I should warn you—driving through snow in the mountains

1

isn't the same as driving through it in Nebraska."

"I feel like I would've been there already if it weren't for that stupid flat tire this morning at my hotel in Denver. And then I had to deal with the creeper from the roadside service company who came to change it. He was like forty-five, but he was totally checking me out."

"Gross," Rebecca said. "He's old enough to be your father."

"Didn't seem to stop him."

"Hey, I'm texting you a list of cabins you could rent for the night along that stretch because some of them won't appear on your GPS. You can't be more than a few miles from Conejos Ranch. If you decide to keep driving, there's a private lodge called Menkhaven-on-the-Conejos. You can probably stay there if the weather gets bad. Or, if you're able to keep going, you'll see signs for the Rainbow Trout Ranch, but it's off the highway a bit."

Megan nodded, as if Rebecca could see her. "Thanks for the info. Now stop worrying."

"It's just ... well, none of these places are Motel 6. They are cabins, and some of them will have steps. I—"

"Don't worry. I've been in a wheelchair all my life. I know how to take care of myself. I'll see you soon. Or I'll call you if I need to pull in somewhere." She ended the call and tossed her phone on the seat next to her.

The snow was falling harder now, making it difficult for Megan to see the road. The terrain had changed from flat open fields to a narrow roadway surrounded by a forest, filled with trees Megan thought might be a combination of pine, fir, and aspen, but as a city girl, she couldn't be sure.

The elevation was changing too. She felt her Ford Explorer, the vehicle her grandparents bought for her and had adapted for her disability, shift gears to accommodate the change. Her ears clogged momentarily and she waggled her jaw back and forth to try to get them to pop. Some form of wildlife scurried behind one of the trees as her car approached. All she could see was its tail. *A possum maybe?*

Seeing the snow and the wildlife was relaxing. She hadn't realized how stressed out she had felt over the last month until that moment. Finals were over. Her rent was paid. And she was finally away from her partying roommates for a while. She couldn't wait to get some downtime with Rebecca—her previous roommate who had quit college a year ago to take over a bed and breakfast in Chama, New Mexico that her aunt willed to her.

Megan's life looked considerably different than Rebecca's, but somehow Rebecca understood her and the obstacles she faced. Since the day they met during freshman year in high school, Rebecca had been her advocate, facing down bullies and helping her make her way down crowded aisles in department stores. Rebecca had even battled with able-bodied restaurant and dollar-store patrons who took handicapped parking spaces because they couldn't be bothered to walk an additional twenty steps.

The truth was, after Megan lost her grandparents—the only parents she ever knew—and then ran through the small inheritance they left her, she entered survival mode. She applied for full and partial scholarships to Creighton University in Omaha and ended up receiving a partial scholarship, which covered close to half her tuition, but not her room and board. So she had to apply for financial aid to cover what her scholarship didn't. She was prepared to make any sacrifice necessary to get her certificate as a dental hygienist or assistant, including sharing a rundown house near campus with three other students. Ramen noodles and the thrift store around the corner became her two best friends, other than Rebecca.

The teasing she endured throughout her life gave her a tough exterior. She knew that, but it was intentional. It's easier to snap at people and keep them at arm's length than to let them take advantage of you, or worse, to mock you.

The snow was falling in sheets now. Megan squinted to try to see the road. *Getting a cabin for the night is going to wipe out any extra money I have in my pocket, but it'll be dark soon and I don't want to drive in this much longer. And I'm thinking the forecasters owe us an apology. There's no way this is only going to amount to three or four inches.*

As she rounded a corner, her front tires slipped ever so slightly. That settled it. She grabbed her phone and scrolled through the list of ranches and inns Rebecca had sent. She had already driven past the Conejos Ranch, so she started watching for Menkhaven-on-the-Conejos. Her cell phone sprang to life with a text message.

"Hope u pulled off by now."

"I'm trying Rebecca, I'm trying," she said out loud.

A few minutes later, she spotted a sign on her left for a place called Mercy Inn. The inn's sign flashed VACANCY. *Hmm. That's not on Rebecca's list, and that makes it the perfect reason to stop here.*

* * *

To Brad Hamilton, Google Earth had made Highway 17 look like

4

something out of a painting. The Conejos River flowed nearly parallel to the highway for a portion of his eastward drive and it nearly killed him to pass all of those prime fly-fishing spots and camping sites. But right now, he was more concerned about the snow that had been falling steadily for the past twenty minutes and sticking to the highway.

He tapped a button on his GPS that he had anchored to his Ford F-150's windshield. The synthesized female voice announced he was 286 miles from his destination: Denver, Colorado. *I can knock that out in the morning, no problem. Time to find a room.* As he searched for motels on his GPS, he noticed a VACANCY sign ahead for a place called Mercy Inn. He glanced at his GPS but didn't see Mercy Inn listed. Maybe the place was new.

Hank Williams Jr. blared from his stereo. He quieted Hank, flipped on his turn signal, and tugged on his baseball cap. The back end of his truck fishtailed as he made the turn, but he pulled safely onto the gravel road leading to the inn. The snow was falling harder now, so finding this place when he did was perfect timing. Just a few feet in front of him, a deer scampered off the road and into thick brush that surrounded both sides of the road.

He followed one set of tire tracks at a snail's pace, making sure he could avoid any of Bambi's friends or family if they decided to jump out in front of him. He passed a cabin, and then another one before he realized Mercy Inn rented cabins as rooms.

I'm going to have to hit this stretch of highway again during the summer so I can go fishing. The river must be full of rainbow trout.

He pulled up to the inn's office, grabbed his duffel bag out of the front seat, and patted his back pocket to make sure he had his wallet. Just as he was about to head inside, a woman in a wheelchair, who looked to be in her early twenties, pushed the door open and began wheeling her way out into the elements. Brad held the door open for her and nodded a greeting.

"What? You've never seen a girl in a wheelchair?" she said.

"I—"

"I've had a bad enough day already, dude. I don't need your pity on top of it." She surveyed the road and apparently decided she could navigate the snow to get back to her vehicle because she wheeled past Brad.

Brad raised an eyebrow. "Ma'am, I don't know what you think you saw in my body language, but you misread me. But if you could use a hand in getting to your cabin, I'd be happy to help."

She spun around to face him and narrowed her eyes. "I've had my fill of creepers for one day."

Brad continued to hold the door open. "Look, we got off on the wrong foot ..."

She wheeled away from him before he could finish, but he would check on her after he got his key. Brad stepped inside the office and closed the door behind him. The scent of pine filled his nostrils, making him feel like he was seven years old again. His father used to take him to Walgreens in Farmington every year in late November. The store always had a huge stash of Christmas trees to pick from in a roped-off section outside. Brad always got to pick the tree he wanted, assuming it met the height limit of the living room.

He glanced around the breakfast nook in search of a tree but didn't spot one. Five or six tables sat on a hardwood floor, and the nook was surrounded by two picture windows that took up the entire wall. They provided a perfect view of the snow.

"It's getting nasty out there, isn't it?"

Brad turned to face the voice and removed his gloves. "Have you heard a weather forecast?"

"We're in for a doozy of a storm—more than a foot of snow, they say. My name is Ray. I assume you're here for a cabin?"

Brad groaned. "More than a foot of snow? But tomorrow is Christmas Eve. What are the chances I'll be able to drive through it tomorrow? I'm headed to Denver."

Ray swooshed his pointer finger back and forth like a windshield wiper. "That's not going to happen. Highway 17 isn't the highest priority when it comes to snow removal. In fact, it's one of the last highways in the area to be plowed."

Brad pursed his lips and reached for his wallet in his back pocket. "I guess I'll need a cabin for a couple of nights then."

"Put your credit card away," Ray said. "We'll settle up when you check out."

Brad nodded a thank you. "My name is Brad, by the way." He extended his hand to Ray.

"Pleased to meet you, Brad. Even though you aren't thrilled about the prospect of staying here longer than you intended, my wife and I will do everything we can to make this a profitable stay for you."

Profitable?

Chapter 2

S arah turned her windshield wipers on high, but the snow was falling so hard that she was having a difficult time seeing Highway 17. She reached for the radio volume dial and turned it down.

Thump. Thump.

Thump. Thump.

Thump. Thump.

Normally, she would have found the rhythm of the windshield wipers soothing, but only if she were on a familiar highway. Highway 17 in southern Colorado was anything but familiar.

Sarah squinted, trying to get a glimpse of what might lay ahead. She couldn't see more than a few feet in front of her car. What she could see, she didn't like. This obscure highway was snow-covered—probably a few inches deep, maybe more—and she couldn't even see a single set of tire tracks.

How could she have allowed herself to end up in this situation? She should have left earlier. She knew snow was possible, but one little unfinished task after another caused her to start ninety minutes later than she planned.

I need to find a motel—any motel will do. Mom will understand if I get in late tomorrow. Why didn't I pay better attention to the weather forecast? Years of seclusion creates bad habits, I guess.

She gripped the steering wheel tighter and took her foot off the accelerator, cutting her speed to forty miles per hour. Ironically, she had been looking forward to seeing this eighty-five-mile stretch of highway more than any other portion of her trip from her home in Farmington, New Mexico to Colorado Springs where her mother had moved recently.

She had seen the majestic mountains in the Springs numerous times, but her best friend, Kim, took a trip last year in which she traveled this same highway and she couldn't stop talking about it.

"About halfway through the drive, you'll wind around several mountains, and if you dare, glance out the window—especially once you get to the plateaus—and you'll see solitary cabins that are set maybe a mile or two off the highway," Kim said one Saturday morning over coffee at Durango Joe's. "If a person made the drive during the winter, it would make for a perfect Christmas card photo."

Sarah's eyes got big. "Sounds magical. On one hand, it sounds like the perfect place to be stranded in a snowstorm. On the other hand, it sounds like the worst place in the world to be stranded in a snowstorm." She tucked a strand of her chin-length, auburn hair behind her ear and took a sip of her skinny mocha latte.

"How much fun would it be to pull off the main road during a snowstorm and be forced to approach one of those cabins?" Kim said. "The family inside would have to take you in. And then you would get to experience an old-fashioned Christmas—one with a real fireplace, and a real Christmas tree, without feeling the pressure to attend work parties or finish last-minute Christmas shopping."

"Umm, you're assuming that an ax murderer or a Unabomber

9

knock-off isn't hiding inside that cabin."

They both laughed, knowing the scenario was too far-fetched to ever become a reality.

Sarah wasn't laughing now.

Music began to fill the car—it was her phone. She knew it was vain, but she had set it to "Romance Me"—one of her biggest hits. It seemed like another lifetime ago but hearing the song every time somebody called her reminded her of the life she left behind. She was glad to have done so, but she needed to keep it alive somehow, if only in her mind. If she didn't, then that period of her life would slip away into a foggy nothingness and she couldn't allow that to happen. She had loved Rick too much to allow that.

She let the phone call go to voice mail. It was probably her mom. She could call her back once she reached a motel.

She turned the radio up and hit the scan button.

"... a good night to stay inside. The forecast for south central Colorado has been updated. Fourteen to sixteen inches of snow is expected by 3:00 o'clock tomorrow afternoon. On the bright side, tomorrow is Christmas Eve, so we will certainly have a white Christmas."

Sarah jabbed the power button, silencing the jovial radio personality. *Great. What are the chances that someone will plow this out-of-the-way highway anytime soon? First things first. Get to a place of safety.*

Suddenly, she saw a neon light, the sign took shape: MERCY INN. She tapped her brakes so she could make the turn, and in an instant, her car was sideways—out of control. Her stomach sank. She grabbed the wheel even tighter. Expecting to make an impact with a tree or a post at any moment, she screamed.

* * *

Megan pulled her Explorer up to THOMAS, the name of her cabin, and turned off her engine. She removed the keys from the ignition and punched a button on her key fob. The door on the passenger side opened, allowing a ramp to deploy. She pushed the toggle switch on the side of her seat, causing her seat to slide back toward the center section of her vehicle.

Once it was in place, she pulled another lever near the toggle switch, and her driver's side seat rotated to a forty-five-degree angle. From there, she was able to transfer to her wheelchair that was waiting for her where the middle section of seats would ordinarily be located. She pushed herself down the ramp, punched a button on the inside of the door frame to retract the ramp, then reached back inside for her suitcase.

The snow was falling harder now. She set her suitcase into her lap and wheeled herself up to the front door of her cabin, sliding her key card for entry. As she crossed the threshold, her suitcase slid off her lap and onto the floor. She cursed and jerked her chair forward, shoving the suitcase out of the way with her lifeless feet. At least she was out of the elements.

Maybe more importantly, she had been able to avoid a religious conversation with Mr. Jordan, one of the inn's owners. As she had checked in, he told her that each of the twelve cabins was named after one of Jesus' disciples.

"That's nice." She smiled, hoping to appease him.

He showed her where her cabin was located on a map and offered to push her there, but she rejected his offer, figuring he would use it as a way to start a conversation about God. As soon as she had avoided him, she ran into the creeper on her way out of the lodge. She certainly didn't want him to know which cabin she was staying in, but her concern seemed foolish now, given that he could see her vehicle and her wheelchair tire tracks leading up to her cabin.

Megan flipped the light switch by the front door. The cabin contained a vanity with a round elegant mirror that went three-fourths of the way up the wall, a writing table that could accommodate her laptop, a double bed in the corner with mahogany posts—a nice touch—a couch, and a flat-screen TV that had to be at least forty-four inches.

She was especially excited about the window at the back of the cabin, thinking she would appreciate the view, but the snow didn't allow her to see more than a couple of feet.

Someone knocked on her door.

She ignored it at first. But whoever it was, knocked again. And again.

Rolling up to the front window, she eased the curtain back a couple of inches and saw the creeper standing there. *Oh, come on. I just want to be left alone.* She answered the door anyway, figuring it was the quickest way to make that happen. "What?"

"I just wanted to make sure you got here safely," he said.

"Well, couldn't you tell by my tire tracks that I did?" She tilted her head. "Look, I don't need any help. And I don't need you checking on me. So please stop."

"Gotcha. I won't bother you again. But I'm in PETER, just two cabins down if you change your mind. My name is Brad, by the way." He extended his hand.

Megan's cell phone rang. "I won't change my mind. And I need to answer that. Goodbye, Brad." She slammed the door.

* * *

"Hey Rebecca, I made it safely," Megan said.

"Where are you?"

"I found a place that wasn't on your list—it's called Mercy Inn. The snow was starting to accumulate, so I took the first place I could find." She cradled her phone to her ear with her shoulder and rolled away from the front door. Eying the couch, she grabbed the TV remote and hit the power button before sliding from her wheelchair onto the cushions.

"Don't take any chances tomorrow. You're way up in the mountains, probably more than 8,000 feet, and snowstorms can appear out of nowhere."

"I'm less than an hour away." Megan flipped her brown hair over her shoulders. "I'll be fine. I feel like I've waited way too long to see you and I can't imagine spending Christmas Eve and Christmas Day here. Did I tell you I've already attracted another creeper?" She began flipping through the channels.

"You what?"

"The dude must be forty. He's staying two cabins down from me and he's already held the door open for me, offered to push me to my cabin, and just a minute ago, he knocked on my door to 'check on me.'" She made air quotes around the phrase.

"Did he make any advances?"

"He's playing the nice guy card. That makes me trust him even less."

"Trust your instincts, girl."

She clicked past CNN, MSNBC, Fox News, CNN Headline News, TBS, and TNT. She stopped on a local channel and silently read the scroll across the bottom of the screen: "If you live in southern Colorado, roads will be completely snow and ice-covered through Christmas Day ... up to fourteen inches of snow is expected ... travel is unadvised ..."

Megan sighed. "Great! The local news is saying we are going to get more than a foot of snow. This is completely unacceptable."

Chapter 3

Alma Jordan stopped wiping one of the tables in the nook and glanced over at Ray, who was seated behind the front counter. "Has the third one arrived yet?"

Ray Jordan looked up from the guest registry book. "She's still out there somewhere." He pointed toward the highway. "Apparently, she's been held up by the storm."

"Are you going through that old registry again?"

Ray flipped a page. "Isn't it incredible to read all of these names? Every one of them has a story about how He intervened, sending them in a new direction."

Alma smiled and nodded. "Truth be told, I go through the registry every year about this time too. I often wonder how everyone is doing, but that's not for us to know." She continued wiping the tables as the coffee maker finished gurgling. She inhaled the aroma. "It's about time to invite the first two arrivals, isn't it?"

"I reckon it is." Ray closed the book and reached for his coat, gloves, and stocking cap. "I'll be back in two shakes."

Alma giggled to herself. Ray could use the most adorable phrases sometimes.

＊ ＊ ＊

By the time Ray reached Brad's cabin, the storm had turned into an all-out blizzard, making it difficult for him to see anything more than just a couple of feet in front of him. Everything was going exactly as planned. He knocked on Brad's door and leaned against the shovel he brought with him.

Brad answered with a granola bar in his hand.

"My wife, Alma, has prepared a few sandwiches and some finger food back at the lodge," Ray said. "We figured you probably hadn't had dinner, given the weather conditions. So consider this your formal invitation to join us for an informal meal."

Brad nodded his appreciation. "Come on in."

Ray stepped inside. "Alma also has some delicious smelling coffee just about ready and I think she even made some chocolate chip cookies for after dinner."

Brad glanced at his granola bar. "Your invitation certainly sounds better than the three-course dinner I had planned: a granola bar, a bag of chips, and a soda. I'm in. Just let me put on my shoes and coat and I'll be right over."

Ray knew Megan wouldn't be as easy to convince, but an angel's job was rarely easy. Megan hadn't made much eye contact and she spoke in hushed tones when she registered, projecting a just-leave-me-alone vibe. She had been hurt in the past—he was sure of it. Getting through to her would require gentleness and patience.

He approached her cabin and began shoveling the gravel path that led to the lodge. Once he was finished, he knocked on her door and tried to catch his breath. Shoveling was harder work than he remembered.

No answer.

He knocked again.

She might need a minute to get back into her wheelchair.

She flung open the door. "I told y—"

Ray held up his hands, still out of breath.

"Oh, I'm sorry, Mr. Jordan. I thought you were somebody else."

"Please, call me Ray. And I just wanted to invite you to dinner in the lodge—nothing fancy—since you probably didn't have a chance to grab anything to eat before you registered. Alma made sandwiches, coffee, and some treats. We would love to have you join us. Otherwise, it's all going to go to waste."

Megan frowned.

"Oh, and don't worry. I already shoveled a path for you to the lodge. I'll hit it again after dinner so you can get back to your cabin."

She shifted in her wheelchair and tried to peer around Ray, as if she were trying to confirm that he had indeed shoveled a path for her. "I appreciate the effort, but don't go to any trouble over me. I'm low maintenance."

"No trouble at all. Alma loves to feed people. Come on over. We'll have a good time getting to know one another."

"I think I'll pass. I'm going to Skype with the friend I was planning to visit over the holidays but probably won't get a chance to now. I just heard that the highway has been closed until further notice."

"Well, if you change your mind, you know where to find us."

* * *

17

Sarah opened her eyes. The airbags in her Escort were deployed, so she had hit something. Her windows were fogged over and she could see her breath. *What happened?* She flexed her arms, then legs. Nothing broken, as far as she could tell. She bounced her shoulders up and down to check her ribs, but they seemed fine. She couldn't taste any blood. That was a good sign. She jerked her rearview mirror in her direction and stared for a few seconds. No damage to her face that she could see.

The last thing she could remember was spinning off the highway. She must have been knocked unconscious by the impact—but impact with what? The passenger's side door was caved in partway. "Please tell me I didn't hit another vehicle."

She unbuckled her seatbelt and wiped away a small patch of condensation from the driver's side window. The steady snowfall had turned into a blizzard so she couldn't see a thing. *Am I in a ditch, or maybe a snowbank? Only one way to find out.*

She yanked the handle on the driver's side door and pushed the door open, not meeting any resistance. She stepped out of her car and crept toward the passenger side. She had made contact with a mile-marker sign. In fact, she knocked it down and it was now sticking out from under her car. Apparently, that's what stopped her from sliding off into the ditch and possibly being injured.

The neon sign.

She spun around in search of Mercy Inn. Despite the blizzard, the neon sign beckoned her from not more than ten feet away.

I wonder if the car will start. She climbed back inside and turned the key. The engine sputtered. On the third try, it almost fired, but it also made an awful noise. Something wasn't right, and since she had no earthly idea about anything that went on under the hood, she'd have to call a tow truck once she got inside.

Looks like I am hoofing it. She grabbed her purse, cell phone, and scarf, then wrapped the scarf around her mouth and nose. *I picked a terrible day to wear loafers.* She opened the trunk to retrieve her suitcase on rollers—which would be of no use in this snow. She would have to carry it.

She followed a set of tire tracks down the gravel road toward the inn. The tracks were nearly filled in, so nobody had come or gone for a while. Snowflakes, which were falling horizontally now, stung her eyes. The snow was maybe eight inches deep, with no signs of stopping. *Thankfully, it isn't deeper. But it is considerably deeper than when I slid off the road, so I must have been out for a while.*

Pain shot through her neck. She set down her suitcase, rubbed the back of her neck with her free hand, and rolled her head in a slow circular motion. *I'll be sore tomorrow. Hopefully, that's the extent of my injuries.* She rubbed her neck one more time and reached for her suitcase, which was heavier than she imagined. Of course, she never had any intention of carrying it.

She thought she saw a light in the distance but she couldn't be sure. Animal tracks appeared on the road, causing her to look to the left and then the right for their owners. She was happy not to find them. But as thick as the trees and brush were, and as heavy as the snow was, one could be hiding nearby. *A rabid raccoon is the last thing I want to encounter tonight.*

The light from the inn grew brighter. A few steps later, she could make out the outline of a building—the office, no doubt. She blinked several times, trying to fend off the snow pellets that continued to sting her face. She wiggled her toes inside her snow-packed loafers, trying to get the feeling back in her feet.

She could find a song in this experience, she was sure of it—if she still actually wrote songs. Even though she had been out of the business for over twenty years, she had never been able to turn off her creative side, as much as she wanted to. She had flirted with the idea of writing music again in recent years, but what would she write about? Her fans knew her for her sappy love songs. And those songs defined her life back then. But the music died the night Rick died in a hotel room from a drug overdose.

The rumors she heard after his death made matters worse. She had never seen any evidence of drug use before that night, and she certainly didn't suspect that he had been cheating on her. But she didn't have the heart to investigate either charge after he died, at least not at first. In fact, she didn't have the heart to do much of anything after he died. But three years after Rick's death, she began asking questions.

Rick's friends confirmed that he was a drug user, but they said he was a functional user—as if that made it better. They suspected his overdose was accidental, and none of them had ever seen him with another woman. In fact, they seemed to go out of their way to try to convince her that he had always been faithful to her and that their love really did warrant the many number one love songs Sarah recorded in the early 1990s.

Rick's best friend, Greg, pulled Sarah aside one night at a mutual friend's birthday party. "He was the same guy you married. He adored you. But he had an addiction he couldn't lick. He was embarrassed by it and just didn't think you would accept it."

What hurt her most was knowing Rick trusted his friends with his struggles more than he trusted her. She would have been shocked by the news, at least initially, but she would have stood by him. She was sure of it. But that was easy to say now.

She was close enough to the office that she could see a couple of men and a woman gathered around a table inside. She opened the door and plopped her suitcase into the entryway, taking in the heat. Oh, the glorious heat.

"Welcome, ma'am, I didn't hear you pull up." The elderly man got up from one of the tables and approached her.

She removed her scarf. "I had an accident on the highway and had to walk from there. It wasn't anything too serious, but I hit a mile-marker sign and now the engine makes an awful noise when I turn the key." She took her shoes off, leaving them on the mat in the entryway to dry out.

An elderly woman approached her. "Are you sure you're okay, dear?"

Sarah rolled her head in a circular motion again. "My neck is a little sore, and I'm sure it'll be worse tomorrow, but other than that, I'm fine."

Alma put an arm around her. "If there's anything we can do for you, dear, be sure to let us know."

"The highway has been shut down through Christmas Day, so you don't need to worry about your car right now. My name is Ray, by the way. I'm one of the co-owners of this inn. And the woman who is hugging on you is my lovely wife, Alma."

They exchanged handshakes.

"I'm Sarah Donaldson, and it looks like I'll need a room for the next couple of nights."

"Sure thing, but first, won't you join us for a bite to eat?" Alma said.

Chapter 4

B rad tugged on his baseball cap, wondering what he should do. He recognized Sarah instantly. Her southern accent and facial features were undeniable. In fact, he didn't like to admit it to his friends, but he had all three of her albums and had even listened to two of them earlier in the afternoon in his truck.

She was Sarah Rose—he was sure of it, but why did she just say her last name was Donaldson? Probably because Sarah Rose was a country music superstar turned hermit after the death of her husband, Rick, in the mid-1990s.

Most of her songs were about Rick. The general school of thought was, Sarah dropped out of the limelight because she couldn't bear the idea of going onstage to sing those songs any longer. It was just too painful. But now, here she was ... standing in front of him, or nearly in front of him.

Don't make a fool of yourself. Play it cool.

Sarah removed her gloves, hat, and coat and handed them to Alma, who was waiting to hang them up for her. After doing so, she waved at Brad.

"This is Mr. Hamilton," Ray said. "He's one of our guests."

Brad stood and extended a hand toward her. "Pleased to meet you, ma'am, but please call me Brad. I already feel old enough."

She shook his hand, making eye contact. "Only if you'll call me Sarah."

He had forgotten what butterflies felt like, until that moment. He used to get them before every game he played in the minor leagues—not because he was nervous to perform in front of fans. Most minor league fans weren't there for the game. They were there for the free t-shirt giveaway and to sing "Take Me Out to the Ball Game."

Instead, he was nervous because every at-bat and every pitch were evaluated, and that information was passed along to the respective big league club. All it took was one report from his manager, hitting coach, or player development rep that said his bat was slowing down and his dream of making it to the big leagues would die. Eventually, that's exactly what happened.

He took a job coaching in the minor leagues for a few seasons, but he was about to begin a new phase of his career as a minor league manager, and he suspected he would get butterflies when he met with the media in Wilmington for the first time. But he knew none of the butterflies would come close to feeling like he did the second he shook Sarah's hand.

"Grab a sandwich and some chips." Alma put a hand on Sarah's shoulder and directed her toward the table with the food on it. "It's nothing fancy, but on a cold snowy night, it's the best I could do on such short notice."

Brad was thankful for the reprieve, and he retreated to his table to finish his meal. Maybe she would join him.

"This looks great, thanks." Sarah made herself a ham and cheese sandwich and grabbed a few chips from the bag. "What is that aroma? Smells like Christmas."

"It's a coffee flavor called 'Christmas Delight,'" Alma said. "It's one of my own concoctions."

"You have your own line of coffee?"

"Don't be too impressed, dear. I just have a local vendor who provides a couple of bags each Christmas season. But I should warn you, if you're counting calories, fat grams, carbs, or anything else, then your diet will be blown to smithereens."

Sarah laughed. It was a soft laugh though—a sad one if Brad was a judge of such things.

"But seriously, who counts calories, fat grams, or carbs during Christmas?" Alma said.

"Good point."

Alma poured Sarah a cup. "Just take a seat anywhere."

She looked at Brad. "Mind if I join you?"

His mouth was full, so he just waved her over.

She took a seat and Alma set her mug in front of her. "So, where were you headed before this storm so rudely interrupted your plans?"

Brad was thankful that she started the conversation. "I live in Farmington, just past the New Mexico border, and I was headed to Denver to spend the holiday with my two children, who really aren't children anymore."

Sarah blinked and pulled her head back in apparent shock. "Farmington?"

"You've heard of it?" He took a bite of his roast beef sandwich and washed it down with a sip of coffee.

"I live there—well, I live on a ranch just outside of Farmington. I moved there ... a long time ago." She sipped her coffee and glanced down at her plate.

Brad had heard the rumors about Sarah living in the area, but he had his doubts, given that he had never actually seen her in town. Of course, she was pretty reclusive, and she moved into the area after he graduated from high school and left to play baseball. As a result, he wasn't in town eight or nine months a year, so it was possible.

"I'm familiar with your story," Brad said. "It's hard not to be, given who you are. Truth be told, I'm a huge fan."

Sarah didn't respond. She popped a chip into her mouth, avoiding eye contact. She took another bite of her sandwich and nodded. "And here I thought my crow's feet, a shorter hairstyle, and over twenty years out of the limelight were an adequate disguise."

"And don't forget your different last name."

She grinned at him. "Well yeah, but clearly that didn't work." She glanced down at Brad's left hand.

Is she checking for a wedding ring?

She took a bite of her sandwich. "The truth is, people still recognize me on occasion, as much as I wish they didn't," Sarah said. "It's not that I'm ungrateful, but when I dropped out of public life, I just wanted to become like everybody else."

Brad nodded. "And here I am going against your wishes. I apologize."

"Thank you, but no apology is necessary. I chose the public life and once you choose it, there is no going back—no matter how hard you try."

* * *

Sarah's cabin—named BARTHOLOMEW—was more than she expected. Nice hardwood floors, a vanity that had to be an antique, a twin bed in the corner with a plush comforter, a fireplace she couldn't wait to get going, and the scent of pine throughout. It even had a table with enough room for four. She plopped her suitcase on the bed and began to unpack, thinking about the life she left behind so many years ago. It was hard not to after Brad recognized her.

She hadn't released any music in twenty-two years. Many country music sensations had come and gone. Her music was rarely played on the radio anymore, except for classic country stations. And the calls for interviews had slowed to a trickle.

It helped that she moved away from Nashville and changed her cell phone number periodically. But a few journalists who were hungry to break a big story still found a way to track her number down on occasion. She never understood how they did it, but she was polite in turning down their interview requests, always ending each call with a request to not call her again—sort of like telling an annoying telemarketer to place her on the do-not-call list. She doubted her request would be honored in either case.

But diehard country music fans still recognized her from time to time. The women who listened to her music back when they were in high school always recognized her. They usually told her that one particular album or another had been the soundtrack of their summers. A few men recognized her too. Most of them seemed harmless enough, but she had encountered her share of crazies over the years too. Unfortunately, that was the price of fame.

She set her laptop on the table and hit the power button. While she waited for it to boot up, she took a few more sips of her second cup of Christmas Delight. It had a hint of peppermint and a blend of other familiar flavors that she couldn't quite put her finger on. Even so, it was the best coffee she had ever tasted. She was going to have to ask Alma where she could buy it.

She called her mom, Abigail, on FaceTime and waited for her to pick up. She chuckled over her mom's recent struggle to understand how to use FaceTime on her new iPad. She would often move her iPad around in an attempt to get a better view of her daughter, failing to understand that she didn't control the camera on Sarah's side.

Her mom's face appeared on her screen. "I'm so happy to hear from you. Is everything okay?"

Mothers never stopped worrying. "I'm fine, but my Escort isn't."

"You got into an accident?"

"It wasn't all that bad. I slid off the road and wrapped my car around a sign, but I was within walking distance of a nice inn. I just got settled into my room."

"Are you hurt?"

"I'm sure I'll be sore, but it wasn't a violent impact." In reality, she couldn't remember the impact, but why worry her mother if she didn't have to?

Abigail's cat, Espresso, jumped in front of the camera. "Mommy hasn't abandoned you, baby. But she needs to talk to your sister for a minute. She was on the way to see us, but is going to be held up because of a snowstorm." Abigail stroked Espresso, who purred her appreciation for the affection.

Sarah loved cats as much as the next girl, but her mom went a bit overboard. She understood it though. Pets are like family, especially when you're alone. Abigail lost her beloved, Harold, eight years ago to prostate cancer. "Actually Mom, we're in the middle of a blizzard and they have already shut down the highway through Christmas Day. Maybe we can make it a late Christmas this year?"

"Isn't there some other route you can take?"

Sarah finished the last of her coffee. "This is a lonesome old stretch of highway and I'm nowhere close to any other highways. Even if I were, I wouldn't be able to get there."

Espresso jumped off the table.

"Well, be safe. We can do Christmas anytime."

The landline in Sarah's room rang. *Who in the world?*

"Will do. Love you, Mom. I'll call you tomorrow."

Sarah ended the FaceTime call and answered the phone.

"Stop by the lodge for breakfast in the morning," Alma said. "And Ray and I will round up something for lunch too. But I'm really calling to invite you to a special Christmas Eve dinner we are preparing for all our guests. We do it every year. Most of our guests don't plan to be here on Christmas Eve, but we like to make the best of it for those who do."

"Thanks for the invitation. I'll let you know tomorrow morning, okay?"

"What's the problem, dear?"

Sarah took a seat on the couch, searching for the right words.

"Are you still there?"

Sarah sighed. "Christmas is just a hard time for me." It was a white lie, but now that her secret was out, she knew one of them—probably Brad—would ask the same question everybody had been asking her since the day she walked off the stage for the last time: Why? Nobody had the right to ask that question. If she wanted to quit, she had every right to.

"Oh, I understand. Christmas is a difficult time for many people. But we would love to have you."

"Okay, we'll see."

Chapter 5

Megan checked her bank balance from her phone, already knowing the approximate number before it appeared: $328.66—which would have been enough for gas, food, and one night in a motel. But now she was going to have to pay for two additional nights at Mercy Inn, which meant she wouldn't be able to afford this trip once the highway reopened. She would have to return to Omaha the day after Christmas without getting to see Rebecca.

How am I going to explain this to her? I can't tell her I'm broke.

Megan's stomach growled. She should have taken Ray up on his offer for dinner. *Maybe I can still grab a plate at the lodge.* If Ray and Alma provided meals for the next two days, she could save a little money, and maybe she could hint at needing a big discount on her room. She knew Rebecca would provide all the meals once she got to Chama. So she just needed enough money for lodging and gas. If everything fell into place, she might still be able to make the trip, but she would be coasting back into Omaha on fumes, in more ways than one.

She bundled herself back up and opened the door. A sharp wind cut into her face as the snow blew sideways. The snow was probably too deep to drive her vehicle back to the lodge, and the path that Ray had shoveled was disappearing. Remembering

MERCY INN: A CHRISTMAS NOVELLA

how difficult it was to get through the couple of inches of snow previously, she went back inside and picked up the phone to dial the office, hoping Alma would pick up.

"Sure honey, I'd be happy to fix you a plate," Alma said. "I'll send Ray over with it right away."

"I'd come and get it myself, but I'm afraid I would get stuck in the snow."

"Don't worry about it. Ray will be there shortly."

"Awesome, thanks."

A few minutes later, Ray delivered a plate that included a cold-cut sandwich, chips, a pickle, and three homemade chocolate chip cookies. He even brought a steamy mug of the most scrumptious smelling coffee ever.

"I can't thank you enough for doing this." Megan pointed toward her table. "You can just set it over there."

"We are happy to be of service."

She followed him. "Since I hadn't planned on staying an extra two nights, it's really going to take a bite out of my budget. But I feel like a meal like this will help."

"We're all pinching pennies these days, so I know what you mean."

She nodded, hoping her hint was sinking in.

"Alma and I will be providing breakfast and lunch tomorrow. Again, it won't be anything fancy, but tomorrow night, all of that changes. Every Christmas Eve, we plan a huge feast for our patrons. I hope you'll join us for all three meals, especially Christmas Eve dinner."

What choice do I have? "I'll be there."

Ray pulled his gloves back on. "Great. I'll shovel the pathway again in the morning so you can get over to the lodge for breakfast. Have a good night."

"You too." She closed the door behind him. At least he didn't try to push religion on her. Maybe she had misjudged him.

She rolled back over to the couch and began flipping through the channels. She stopped on HBO when she saw that *Gravity*, starring George Clooney and Sandra Bullock, was just beginning. She intended to see it at the theater when it came out a few years ago, but her full-time schedule at school combined with the twenty hours she was putting in at the coffee shop didn't allow much time for movies. Plus, who had twenty dollars to spend in a movie theater?

She grabbed the comforter off the bed and curled up on the couch to watch it. Tears rolled down her eyes as Bullock's character, Ryan Stone—a medical engineer who was on her first space expedition—confessed that nobody would miss her if she were to die in space. Ryan lost her son when he was just four years old, which angered her at first, but then she went numb, shutting out every person around her. When the mission went haywire, Ryan fought to survive, realizing she no longer wanted to shut people out. She wanted to begin living again.

Megan could relate. She never knew her biological parents. Her father took off shortly after she was born, and her mother died of pancreatic cancer when she was just two. Her grandparents on her mother's side did a phenomenal job in raising her, even though it couldn't have been easy for them to manage her cerebral palsy. They were getting up there in years and struggled with her wheelchair, her physical therapy, her multiple surgeries, and then the long recovery periods afterward. But they were gone now and nobody would miss her if she died.

* * *

Brad rolled over in bed and checked the clock: 6:14 a.m. Not even five hours of sleep. Megan thought he was a creeper, and he couldn't help but wonder if he came off like a crazed fan with Sarah. But why did either perception bother him so much?

Coffee. He needed coffee.

He fumbled around in the dark, looking for a light switch by his bed. Once he found it, he stumbled toward the kitchen, shuffling his feet on the wood floors. Soon, the coffee pot gurgled to life. He drained his cup and jumped into the shower. Afterward, he threw on a pair of jeans and a white t-shirt. He ran a comb through his casual, wavy brown hair before finally doing what he had been thinking about all night—listening to all three of Sarah's albums back-to-back-to-back. He didn't know exactly what he was listening for—maybe to see if he had missed anything.

Sarah's self-titled debut album in 1989 launched her to number one on the charts. She had the perfect combination of personality, talent, and looks, and she took the country music world by storm. In fact, her music crossed over and she sat atop the pop charts too, which didn't exactly endear her to the Nashville elite. Her first single, "I Wrote You a Love Song," was a catchy little number you only had to hear once before you could sing along with the chorus.

With his coffee in hand, Brad plopped down on the couch, put his feet on the coffee table, inserted his earbuds, and punched the play button on his iPhone, listening to the song, singing along with it. He wasn't ashamed of knowing the words. Sarah had recorded this album when he was a teen himself and the songs were popular during his senior year in high school, back when he began dating his first love, Karen. Times were simpler then. The great thing about music was, it could transport you to the best times of your life and let you linger there for a while.

The second song, "All Cried Out," was a big, sweeping production about two young lovers who were separated by circumstances. Brad closed his eyes and whispered the lyrics. It was the perfect contrast to the first song on the album, since young love often fades, but the time in between would never be forgotten by either participant. That's why he always thought this song belonged at the end of the album.

He listened to the song a second time, wondering why Sarah would include a breakup song on the album, given that her marriage to Rick was still in its infancy. *Did she include the song because her record company thought it would be a hit, or was there trouble in paradise?* A quick Google search revealed that someone else had written the song, which was odd since Sarah was known for writing most of her own material. *This must have been the record company's idea.*

Three songs later, he was lost in the music, forgetting about his coffee and forgetting about being stranded for the holidays. For a brief moment, he even forgot about the possibility that Sarah might want to keep him at arm's length. Instead, he was back at Hutchison Stadium on a particular Friday night at the Farmington High School football game in which he slipped his arm around Karen for the first time. She leaned into him, so his gamble paid off. They were inseparable after that.

But Brad had a problem.

A scout for the Philadelphia Phillies showed up at one of his baseball games that same year to watch the best pitcher in the league, but Brad caught his eye at second base. The scout told him he was impressed with the way Brad handled himself around the bag—his positioning and his ability to turn the double play, while always thinking one step ahead. And he complimented the way he handled the bat in the two hole, as well, noting that he advanced runners twice on sacrifices to the right side of the infield.

"You've got good instincts, kid, and those can't be taught," the scout said. "You're also fundamentally sound. I don't know if your offensive numbers are good enough to be drafted, but don't give up hope. If you aren't drafted, we will probably be in touch."

The scout was right. Nobody drafted him, so Plan B—college—was back on the table. But a day after the draft ended, his phone rang and the Phillies offered him a $5,000 signing bonus with the chance to play rookie ball right away. He wouldn't make a lot of money. In fact, he would just barely get by, just like everybody else in rookie ball, with the exception of the high draft picks. But he was being given the opportunity to play professional baseball for a living, no matter how meager his paycheck might be.

Meanwhile, Karen headed for the University of Denver in the fall to pursue a career in law. Brad visited her in Denver whenever his crazy schedule would allow, and after she graduated, they were married and had two children: Ryan and Amy.

But as Brad bounced from one organization to the next in pursuit of making it to the big leagues, Karen began to hint that it was time to hang up his cleats and find a job that would allow him to be home more often. He ignored her hints and chased his dream well into his thirties. He returned home during the All-Star break one season and Karen was gone. She had left him for another man.

Looking back, he understood her decision, but that didn't mean the betrayal didn't cut deep. It most certainly did—deep enough to keep him from committing to anyone else.

In fact, he had never felt that spark with anybody else … until he shook hands with Sarah. He was near the end of her second album, *An Old Fashioned Love Letter*—an album that was true to Sarah's reputation, in that most of the songs on the album were indeed sappy love songs—when the phone rang. It was Alma, reminding him she was serving breakfast in forty-five minutes. He finished listening to the album and began listening to Sarah's third release, *Not as Simple as It Seems*—a more mature, reflective album.

He poured a fresh cup of coffee and sipped from it as the third track on the album, "Unfinished Love," began to play.

> *As the years roll by,*
> *I'm learning it's hard to satisfy,*
> *my dreams about love as a little girl.*
> *Maybe I was just a dreamer,*
> *maybe even a naive believer,*
> *but I had to find out for myself.*

A quick search revealed that Sarah had written this song. In fact, she wrote every song on her third album. Was this her way of saying her love for Rick had matured to the point that she realized he couldn't be her sole source of happiness? Or again, was there trouble in paradise? He chided himself for thinking the latter. Several top forty hits later, another seemingly out-of-place track called "Lonely Imitations" began to play.

Brad had noticed these introspective songs in the past, but he never thought much about them. But for the first time, he realized that none of these songs had been released as singles, and consequently, none of them had been hits. Maybe they weren't the products of her record company. Maybe they only tolerated these types of songs because she was cranking out so many love songs that became hits.

He finished listening to the album and removed his headphones, considering his next move. It's not that he lacked confidence or experience in attracting a woman he was interested in. But this felt different and it wouldn't be as easy as slipping his arm around her at an opportune moment.

Chapter 6

Sarah brushed the snow out of her hair with her hands and paused outside the lodge. She couldn't bear the thought of spending the holidays alone in her cabin, so she decided to take a chance. She let out a breath and opened the door.

Mannheim Steamroller's version of "Joy to the World" played in the background on a stereo at the check-in counter. She caught a whiff of what she believed to be bacon, French toast, and maybe scrambled eggs. She would gain five pounds before she got back on the road, but it was Christmas Eve. Why not indulge?

Ray greeted her. "You made it!" He got up from his seat behind the counter. He reminded Sarah of the way men used to stand every time a woman entered a room in her grandparents' generation. She smiled at him. "How are you feeling? Are you sore from the accident?"

"I'm certainly stiff." She rolled shoulders. "And my neck is sore, but I'm fine." She caught sight of a woman in a wheelchair in the nook. *Must be another stranded traveler.*

"Well, if you need anything, just let us know."

"Will do. Thanks."

"Grab a mug and help yourself to the coffee," Ray said.

"Breakfast will be ready momentarily."

The woman waved Sarah over to her table and introduced herself. Sarah took a seat and they traded travel stories. Megan was pleasant but guarded. Sarah could relate. *Why put yourself out there if you don't have to?*

Alma appeared with two plates full of food. "Here you go. Hope you enjoy it."

"I certainly didn't expect gourmet meals," Megan said.

Alma blushed. "Oh, stop. This is hardly gourmet. This is what Ray and I would be eating anyway. I just made more than usual. We're glad to have you folks with us for Christmas, even though it wasn't in your original plans."

The door opened and Brad stepped inside.

Megan turned away.

"Do you know him?"

"We've met." Megan put her head down, doused her scrambled eggs with pepper, and dug in.

Brad had the opposite effect on Sarah. At first, she thought he might be an overzealous fan, but her fear quickly dissipated. His use of the word "ma'am" when they first met, combined with his tattered baseball cap, knowledge about country music, and his blue eyes—something about his eyes—were working their magic on her, even though she didn't want to admit it. Deep down, he was a country boy.

Alma waved Brad over. "Perfect timing. I'll have your plate right out." She disappeared into the kitchen.

Brad took his time at the coffee pot before finally taking a seat at the table farthest away from Sarah and Megan.

He must have had a run-in with Megan.

Alma returned with a plate full of food. "Why are you sitting way over there? Come on over here and join the rest of us."

38

Brad pursed his lips for a couple of seconds, then picked up his plate and joined Sarah and Megan. "I didn't mean to be rude."

Sarah noticed that he avoided eye contact with Megan as he took a seat at their table.

Alma wiped her hands on her apron. "It's just the five of us for the next two days, so we might as well get cozy. Ray and I are looking forward to spending Christmas with you." She leaned against the back of Sarah's chair, as if for emphasis.

Sarah managed a weak smile.

"I'll leave the three of you alone to enjoy your breakfast." Alma disappeared.

Where did Ray go? If Sarah didn't know better, she would think Ray and Alma were up to something. It almost felt like a setup. She had certainly walked into her share of those over the years, hosted by well-meaning friends who just wanted to see her move on with her life. But how could that be the case? The three of them were virtual strangers to Ray and Alma.

"You'll never guess what I did this morning," Brad said to Sarah.

Sarah raised her eyebrows.

"I listened to all three of your albums."

Megan looked up. "Wait, you recorded three albums?"

"It was a long time ago."

Brad removed his baseball cap and scratched the back of his head, placing his cap in his lap. "But it was great music. You were on the radio every other song, or so it seemed, when I was in high school." He shoveled several bites of food into his mouth before speaking again. "But I imagine you get tired of hearing people say that." He glanced up, as if to gauge her reaction.

She tucked a strand of hair behind her ear. It flopped back into place a second later. "It doesn't happen nearly as often as it used to."

Megan's eyes grew wide. "Have I ever heard of you?"

"I recorded under the name Sarah Rose."

* * *

"I'll Be Home for Christmas" by Elvis played softly in the background while the lights on the Christmas tree in the den—just a few feet from the nook—seemed to dance, reminding Megan of Christmases past, when she was a little girl. Her grandparents always made sure to go all out for the holidays to make her feel as normal as possible—well, as normal as a child can feel whose parents have died.

"No way!" Megan said. "I remember singing your songs when I was a little girl. My grandparents recorded a video of me singing 'November Love.' My pigtails bounced all over the place."

Sarah smiled. "Thanks for making me feel ancient."

Alma stopped back by the table a few minutes later. "Anybody want seconds? We have plenty of food. Or maybe a refill on your coffee?"

"I'll take a refill," Megan said. She handed Alma her mug. "Thanks."

"Anybody else?"

Brad and Sarah indicated they were good.

"When I finish up in the kitchen, Ray and I have a getting-to-know-you game we like to play with guests at this time of year.

40

Why don't you move into the living room after you're done? You'll find lots of comfortable seating over there."

Megan closed her eyes momentarily. *Great. My options are to either go back to my room and spend the rest of Christmas Eve by myself or to go to the living room and play some lame game.* She had to admit, though, that getting to know a celebrity in such an environment would be pretty cool.

Fifteen minutes later, after everybody finished eating, Megan unlocked her wheels and pushed herself back from the table. Brad and Sarah followed her to the den. Megan transferred herself to the couch and Sarah sat down on the opposite end. Brad chose a brown, high-backed chair that sat at an angle to them. The furniture formed a U-shape facing a pane-glass window that allowed them to see the snow. It was still coming down.

Sarah took a sip of her coffee. "As much as I hate to admit it, the snow is beautiful."

Alma returned with Megan's refilled mug and handed it to her. "The radio says we have nearly a foot on the ground so far, with more to come. The announcer also said forecasters are keeping an eye on another front that is coming together and could dump another six to eight inches tomorrow." She smirked.

I can't be stuck here past Christmas. And why is she smirking?

"You must be a Christmas person," Brad said to Alma.

"You could say that."

Brad nodded. "Did you say we are the only three residents who are staying here right now?"

"We usually only have a few with us for the holidays. I can only remember one other year, maybe 1984 or '85, when guests were stranded here due to a blizzard. Most years, we

41

accommodate family Christmas parties, class reunions, or tired business people without any family to celebrate with.

"Class reunions? At Christmas?" Megan said.

Ray, who had just finished getting a fire going in the fireplace, took a seat in a rocking chair with his back to the fire. "It doesn't happen often, but you'd be surprised. I think some plan class reunions at Christmas to avoid having to travel to be with extended family, but that's just a gut feeling. The holidays are hard for some people—most people, I think."

"So, what's the game you want us to play?" Sarah said.

Ray held a stack of index cards in his hand. Most were yellowed and frayed. "We call it Nicebreaker. It's just a nice way to get to know each other a little better. Might as well, since we are going to be spending the next two or three days together, right?"

Megan tucked her hands under her legs and bit her lower lip.

Ray shuffled the index cards. "There really aren't any rules, per se. Just take four index cards, keeping them face down so you cannot see the questions. Once everybody has his or her cards, we'll take turns asking each other the questions. You don't have to ask people in any certain order, but you can only choose each person once."

Megan raised her eyebrows. "That sounds like a rule to me."

"I guess it is, but I did add 'per se.'"

"I feel like that's a loophole," Megan said.

Alma chuckled and took a seat in a rocking chair next to Ray. "Don't forget, they have to name the person they want to ask the question *before* they flip the card over."

Ray nodded. "I always forget to mention that."

"It's a fun little twist to the game. And that way, nobody can get upset with the questioner."

"So now there are two rules?" Megan said.

"You, dear, are a stickler. I like that. Hold his feet to the fire. Next year, he'll know better than to say there aren't *any* rules."

"Take a Walk through Bethlehem," by Trisha Yearwood played in the background. Megan remembered her grandparents listening to this album every year. On the original album cover, Yearwood had big '80s hair—even though it was 1994. When the album was re-released a few years later, somebody must have decided a more modern look might sell more albums, so Yearwood's picture was replaced by one with big wavy hair. The original cover would always be Megan's cover of choice. She hummed along to the song.

They passed the index cards around and each person took four.

"Okay, ladies first," Ray said. "Why don't you start, Megan?"

"My first question is for Sarah." Megan flipped the first card. "1 Corinthians 7:7 says each person has his own gift from God. What is your gift and how are you using it right now to help others?"

Sarah just stared at Megan.

Chapter 7

*S*o much for the warm-up questions. Sarah looked down at her lap and clasped her hands. "I imagine all of us have more than one gift. My primary one has always been music. It came naturally to me—both in writing lyrics and then performing those songs onstage. But that phase of my life came to an end when my husband died. We had only been married two years." *No need to drag his name through the mud by adding details about his death.*

Alma pursed her lips. "I thought you looked familiar. You're Sarah Rose, aren't you?"

Sarah nodded and took a deep breath. When Alma didn't press any further, she decided to ask her own question. "Can a gift be seasonal? Who's to say we're supposed to use the same gift our entire lives, right?"

"Don't worry about answering these questions perfectly," Ray said. "They are only intended to help us get to know you better, and maybe help you learn something about yourself. You can say as much, or as little, as you want."

"*Now* you tell me," Sarah said.

Everybody laughed.

But Sarah couldn't shake either question. If her music was a gift, then maybe God gave it to her for reasons beyond herself.

She had heard from fans over the years about how one of her songs was the soundtrack for their wedding video, or about how one of them got someone through a difficult time. She had always considered that a byproduct of the music, not the reason for it.

How could words she jotted down in a notebook on a tour bus or in a motel room mean so much to so many people? And what did that mean in the big picture? Was she responsible for using her gift forever?

Even if she were to begin writing new material, she would have to deal with the same obstacle every artist with a successful backlist faced—her fans would want to hear their old favorites. She could not sing those songs again. She could barely listen to them on the radio now when a fan requested one, often choosing to flip to a different station.

"Can I just plead the fifth on this one? I mean, I can't really answer the question because I've never thought about my music as a gift to be used to help others as much as I saw it as a means to express myself. Even if I never had the chance to sing for thousands of fans, I would have written the songs anyway ... because I had to."

"That's fine, dear." Alma rocked back and forth, seeming to be content with letting Sarah squirm. "Really, it is."

"Okay, my turn." Sarah decided to move on, choosing Ray to answer her first question. "What is your second biggest life-defining moment, and how did it shape everything that followed it? And, if you had it to do all over again, would you make the same decision?"

"All of that fit on one card?" Brad said.

Sarah nodded. "Barely."

"Oh, that's a good one," Megan said. "Who came up with

these questions?"

"It was a team effort, dear," Alma said. "Ray and I wrote the original questions, but every year we ask the participants to write one of their own questions. That's why some of the cards are so beat up, while other cards look so new."

"Great idea," Brad said. "Sort of makes me want to come back next year to see who gets my question."

"You're welcome to, dear," Alma said.

Dean Martin's voice filled the den. "Let It Snow, Let It Snow, Let It Snow" seemed to be the perfect song for the moment. Sarah's mother, Abigail, used to play this song over and over every Christmas.

She could still see her mom hovering over the old stereo, placing the LP on the turntable, and then hearing that distinct scratching noise as she set the needle into the groove. She loved that noise. It was the reason she insisted that her record company release all three of her albums on vinyl as well as CD and audiotape. They threw a fit, but she didn't care. Modern technology may have improved the clarity of sound, but in so doing, it removed some of the beautiful nuances of older technology.

"My second biggest life-defining moment was opening this lodge with my beloved wife so we could have nights like this." Ray nodded at Alma. "People come here as strangers, but leave as friends. We always intended for this to be more than just a place to lay your head for the night. We wanted to make a difference."

"Aww, that's sweet." Megan tilted her head. "But if that was your second biggest life-defining moment, then what was your first?"

Ray chuckled. "No fair asking a follow-up question."

"For a game with no rules, you sure have a lot of rules."

He shrugged.

"Am I up next?" Brad asked.

Ray nodded.

"This one is for Sarah."

* * *

"What is your most embarrassing hairstyle and what made you change it?" Brad frowned. *That is the worst question ever.*

Sarah ran a hand through her hair. "I didn't see that one coming." She laughed.

"Inquiring minds do want to know," Alma said.

Everybody, except Mcgan, laughed. She cocked her head to one side. "Is that something from the old days?"

Ray leaned forward. "Something like that."

"Without a doubt, my most embarrassing hairstyle was in the mid-'80s. I was thirteen or fourteen at the time. My brother once said I used so much hair spray that he had to dodge flies that were suspended in mid-air when he went into the bathroom after one of my grooming sessions—and they really were sessions. My friends were all in when it came to piling our hair as high and wide as it would go. And it certainly didn't hurt that all of the cute boys liked the look."

Brad recalled seeing many photos and videos of Sarah from those days and he had to agree—that '80s poofy hair look that females embraced always did the trick for him.

"Do you have any pictures from those days?" Alma asked. "I would love to see them."

47

"I could check Google images on my phone," Megan said. "I'm sure I could find plenty of them."

"That won't be necessary! Unfortunately, I have one right here." Sarah picked up her phone and began flipping through her gallery. "But if I agree to show it to you, no laughing!"

Megan scooted toward Sarah. "No promises, but I'm dying to see it." She hovered over the screen, watching Sarah's other personal photos whiz by. "Wait, I just saw a picture of two baked potatoes, side by side. What's up with that?"

* * *

"Long story, but I promise to explain it to you if I get a question about why a person might have photos of vegetables on her phone."

Memories of a lazy Saturday evening came flooding back into Sarah's mind. Rick had grilled steaks and baked potatoes that evening. As they were sitting down on the floor at the coffee table in front of the couch to eat dinner and watch *Fried Green Tomatoes*, Sarah was overwhelmed with the feeling that she was living the dream. She was young, married to the only man she had ever loved—one who not only tolerated chick flicks, but secretly admitted to enjoying them, her first album had gone platinum, and her second was climbing the charts. Life couldn't be better.

She had to capture the moment. She paused the movie, sprang to her bare feet, and grabbed her 35mm camera from the bedroom. She returned with a clean plate from the kitchen and snatched the baked potatoes from both plates, setting them on

48

the clean plate.

"Have you lost your ever-loving mind?" Rick said.

"Do you know how a common man is described as a meat and potatoes sort of guy?"

Rick nodded his head.

"I like common," she said. "It makes me feel safe."

"Okay." Rick raised his eyebrows.

"We both already took a bite out of our steaks, but the potatoes are untouched. I just thought they would be a great symbol of the perfectly common day I never want to forget."

Rick nodded, as if he understood. She suspected that he actually did. They were both a bit corny. It was one of the reasons they were attracted to each other. She knew nobody would ever understand the significance of such a photo if they came across it, but she didn't care.

* * *

"No fair," Megan said. "I want to know the potato story."

Sarah kept scrolling, ignoring Megan's request. "Okay, here it is ..."

"Whoa, check this out, you guys." Megan snatched the phone from Sarah's hands and turned it around for the whole world to see.

"How did you get your bangs to stand up like that?" Brad said. "Is that the magic of Aqua Net?"

"Aqua Net was for old ladies. We used Rave."

"Ahh."

Over the Rhine's "All I Ever Get for Christmas is Blue"

began to play. Brad had heard the song before, but he never understood the allure of listening to a song about being blue at Christmas. Besides, didn't Elvis have the corner on that market?

"What made you move away from that hairstyle, dear?" Alma said.

"Did you *see* the picture?"

Everybody laughed.

"Point taken. I guess I'm next." Alma made eye contact with everyone before finally blurting out a name. "Megan." She turned the card over. "How has your biggest tragedy made you stronger?"

Chapter 8

Megan scooted back to her side of the couch. She settled in and sat all the way back, keeping a stoic face. If she didn't know better, she would say she had been set up. How could the girl in the wheelchair get that question?

"You don't have to answer if you don't want to," Sarah said.

Megan was in no hurry to respond. "Mind if I get a refill on my coffee?" she asked Alma, who was happy to oblige.

The steam spiraled heavenward from Megan's mug as Alma poured it. Megan thanked her and took a sip. She made eye contact with Alma, who had a motherly spirit about her.

"O Christmas Tree" by Kenny G played in the background and it brought back such sweet memories.

"This song reminds me of Christmas with my grandparents when I was little," she began. "They raised me. My father took off shortly after I was born and my mother died of pancreatic cancer when I was just two."

She paused for a few seconds. "Anyway, My grandparents really did Christmas right. The tree always had plenty of presents under it. They played Christmas music the entire month of December and they loved this Kenny G album. Grandma made the best chocolate chip cookies in the world and then she hid them so we wouldn't eat them all in one sitting. And Grandpa, well ... I feel like he was the primary offending cookie eater." Megan smiled at the thought of her grandfather.

She traced the top of her mug with her forefinger and her smiled faded. "But they both passed away within just a few months of one another last year, making the Christmas season ... less than perfect."

This was way more than she intended to share. But besides Rebecca, she didn't have anybody else to talk to about this stuff. Megan felt like she could trust Alma, who was the grandmotherly type. Ray seemed to genuinely care about her too. Even Sarah was taking an interest. The jury was still out on Brad. He was clearly fixated on Sarah, which made him less creepy, but who could blame the guy? Apparently, he was clueless about Sarah being damaged goods. Besides, as cute as Brad was, Sarah was way out of his league. He had no shot with her.

Nobody seemed to be in a hurry for her to answer the question Alma had asked her. If she told them her story, they would have sympathy for the wheelchair-bound girl who had been bullied most of her life and then withdrew into her own little world, but she didn't want sympathy. She wanted a group of friends who could see past her wheelchair and her tough exterior. Could she really find that among strangers who were thrown together by a snowstorm?

Reba McEntire's rendition of "O Holy Night" filled the room. Alma began to sing, softly at first.

O holy night!
The stars are brightly shining
It is the night of the dear Savior's birth

52

Long lay the world in sin and error pining
Till He appeared and the soul felt its worth

Ray joined in, harmonizing with Alma.

The thrill of hope the weary soul rejoices
For yonder breaks a new and glorious morn

Sarah and Brad sang the chorus. Megan followed suit.

Fall on your knees
Oh hear the angel's voices
Oh night divine
Oh holy night when Christ was born
Oh night divine
Oh holy night when Christ was born

Megan didn't know much about holiness, but she had little doubt that she had just experienced a holy moment—one that allowed for silence, at least for a little while longer.

"I haven't sung a Christmas carol since I don't know when," Sarah said.

"My wife and I used to sing them with our kids when they were small, but it's been a long time for me too." Brad shook his head. "As a baseball player, I missed a lot of milestones in the lives of my kids—birthdays, first steps, first words, the first day of school each year, but I was always home during the holidays and we really lived it up. Karen cooked all sorts of treats that we inhaled the minute the oven door opened. And I hung enough lights on our house each year to make Clark Griswold jealous."

"Who is Clark Griswold?"

Snickers all around.

Megan really didn't know.

"Just some goofy character from a Christmas movie that was popular long, long ago," Sarah said.

Nobody meant any harm. But as the youngest person in the group, she was the odd person out—just as she had been her entire life. "Maybe I should finally answer the question Alma asked me."

Silence.

She dropped her gaze. "You might think my biggest tragedy is being in this." She reached over and touched the arm of her wheelchair at the end of the couch. "But that really isn't a tragedy—at least for me. It's all I have ever known. The tragedy has been the way I was bullied as a young girl for being in the chair." She paused.

Now it was Sarah's turn to scoot over. She placed a hand on Megan's knee.

"Why would a perfectly able-bodied person block the aisles at school when they saw me coming? All I was trying to do was get down the hallway, like everybody else. And why would they whisper about me as I forced my way through? And what would make them giggle and point at me? Why is any of this acceptable behavior?"

"It's not—not by a long shot," Brad said. He had fire in his eyes. It was the first time she'd seen that from him.

Everybody else nodded in agreement. Sarah patted her knee.

No platitudes. Hmm. Didn't expect that. But we'll see how they respond to this.

* * *

"As for how my biggest tragedy has made me stronger ... it hasn't. And I honestly don't see how it would even be possible for it to make me stronger." Megan stared at Alma as if to challenge her or anybody else in the room to say anything different. "Every snicker, every name they called me, every person who blocked my path, every whisper behind my back stole something from me—my pride, my dignity, my desire to try to make new friends. How can any of that make me stronger?"

Ray knew that the questions needed to do the work. No need to try to force the issue with follow-up questions, or worse—trying to supply overly simplistic answers. The first round of questions usually made participants uncomfortable, but if they stuck around, they usually stayed for the duration. He and Alma had the benefit of a snowstorm on their side this year. The chosen guests could elect to stay in their cabins for the next two days, watching movies, reading, or Skyping with friends if they wanted to, but the human spirit cries out for community. *After all, the Father himself is three-in-one.*

"There's no right or wrong answers here, dear." Alma rocked back and forth with her hands folded in her lap. "And it's fine to disagree with the premise of the question. We really just want to get to know you. You've let your guard down by telling us what you've had to face because you're in a wheelchair and I think I can speak for all of us in saying we are honored to hear your story. I know it probably feels like it's too little too late, but don't give up on humanity. My guess is, you're in the beginning stages of making lifelong friendships right here, right now.

Megan dropped her gaze into her lap, seeming to fight back tears as Sarah placed an arm around her and drew her close.

Ray loved Alma's patience. He couldn't imagine hosting

people every year without her by his side. "I guess it's my turn to ask the next question, right?"

Alma nodded.

Ray tapped the card on top of his stack. "Brad, you're next."

Megan looked up. "About time." She wiped a tear from her cheek and tried to conceal a laugh.

"What is the first prop that comes to mind from your favorite TV show, and what significance does it symbolize in your life?"

"Getting a little philosophical, aren't we?" Brad crossed his legs and leaned back in his chair with his hands behind his head to stare at the ceiling. "The first part of the question is an easy one—my favorite TV show right now is *Duck Dynasty* … and my favorite prop from that program is Uncle Si's beat-up old green tea glass. The dude carries it around with him everywhere. In one episode, he says he carries two things with him at all times—his tea glass and his Bible. Presumably, he carries around that humongous jug of tea too, otherwise, the tea glass wouldn't do him much good."

"Finally—a reference from my era," Megan said.

Ray made a mental note. This was the first time Megan showed any sign of loosening up.

"I love Uncle Si, but who doesn't, right?" Brad said.

"Do you remember the episode he claimed his hands were 'legal weapons'?" Megan said. "Or the episode he learned about YouTube and then wasted the entire workday in front of the computer watching videos, which gave him the idea that he should make his own golf video? Remember how terrible he was?"

The entire room erupted. As it began to die down, Bobby Darin was just hitting the chorus for "O Come, All Ye Faithful."

O come, let us adore Him,
O come, let us adore Him,
O come, let us adore Him,
Christ the Lord.

They didn't sing this time. Instead, everybody stopped to listen. The group that started as individuals was beginning to become one.

* * *

Megan was the first to break the silence. "You haven't told us why Uncle Si's tea glass means something to you, or what it symbolizes."

Brad nodded. "In one episode, he explained why the glass was so important to him. His mother sent it to him in a care package when he was serving in Viet Nam. It symbolized home for him, no matter how far away he might be. Farmington will always be home for me, even though my profession has taken me all over the country."

"What do you do for a living?" Ray said.

"I was a minor league baseball player." Brad massaged the back of his neck. He always hated this conversation. "I never made the big leagues. A few years ago, I retired and took a job coaching in rookie ball. This off-season, I was hired to manage a team in the lower levels of the minor leagues in Wilmington, Delaware. I start in a couple of months, when spring training opens."

"So Uncle Si's tea glass means something to you because you

rarely get back home, even though you would like to?" Sarah said.

"I failed to mention that I married my high school sweetheart, Karen, shortly after graduation. I won't get into that right now, but in our first year of marriage, while she was away at law school in Denver and I was in my first year of pro ball, she sent me one of those his and hers lockets—the ones with two halves of a heart. I never wore it—the guys would have teased me mercilessly—but I carried it with me because it felt like home. I guess you could say it was my tea glass."

Chapter 9

So, did Karen get tired of him being on the road most of the year? Did he fool around on the road? Sarah wouldn't be the one to ask such things. Not yet, at least.

"I should say that Karen and I had two children: Ryan and Amy," Brad said. "I missed far too much of their lives chasing my own dream. If I had it to do over again, I would choose a different path."

At least he was being honest.

Johnny Cash was up next. Sarah recognized this particular version of "Silent Night" from his *Christmas with Johnny Cash* album that was released in 2003, the year he died. It contained songs he recorded from the early 1960s to 1980. *Rolling Stone* magazine named it the 15th best Christmas album of all time. She loved how they described it, saying he gives the songs "a rough honesty that adds to their redemptive power."

If only the critics had been so kind about her music. But she was no Johnny Cash.

Everybody paused to listen.

When the song was over, Ray patted Alma's knee. "Why don't you start round two?"

"Since we are supposed to ask a different person each round, how are we going to keep track of all this?" Megan said.

"We're on the honor system," Ray said. "And don't worry, if you try to ask somebody a second question, he or she will be quick to remind you. Nobody wants to be on the hot seat more often than necessary." He chuckled and then nodded in Alma's direction.

"I'm thinking, I'm thinking," she said. "Don't rush me."

"Heaven forbid."

"I'm pretty sure it does."

Sarah was drawn to this couple—their obvious admiration for one another, their banter, the way they worked as one unit. It was impressive to see.

A cat jumped into Sarah's lap. "What in the world?" She nearly spilled her coffee.

Alma clapped her hands in excitement. "Oh, that's Snowball the Lodge Cat. You can call him Snowball for short. He's been with us for thirteen years. He is shy at first, so he's probably been hiding. But since we've settled down, he decided now would be the time to meet you."

Snowball—who was aptly named, given his long white poofy fur—spun around in circles on Sarah's lap, trying to find a place to get comfortable, before finally plopping down and curling up.

"He adopts one resident every Christmas," Alma said. "Looks like you're it this year."

Sarah stroked his fur from head to tail.

"Oh, it's a bonus round!" Ray said.

"What does that mean?" Megan said.

"The first person whose lap Snowball falls asleep in has to answer a bonus question," Ray said. "All in good fun, of course."

Sarah groaned.

"For the bonus round, I draw an index card from the pile of unused questions," Ray said. He grabbed the top card and flipped it. "What is the craziest thing you ever did for love?"

"Are you sure there's not another question in there about hairstyles?" Sarah rearranged herself on the couch, being careful not to rouse Snowball, all the while noticing the nervous laughter in the room. *Might as well jump right into the story.* "Rick and I were high school sweethearts in Jackson, Mississippi. He was the pursuer in the relationship, and I was happy to be pursued by him." Her cheeks grew warm. "Too much information?"

"No way," Megan said. "Spill it."

"He was cute as all get out, athletic, and he had a sense of justice about him that I was just drawn to. If he saw one of his football teammates, or anybody for that matter, picking on another kid, he wouldn't tolerate it."

"What I wouldn't have given for someone like that at my high school," Megan said.

Sarah nodded. "I wish you would have had someone like Rick on your side too." She let the sentiment linger before continuing. "Rick and I rarely fought, but during our first major disagreement, he pulled away from me, emotionally. We hadn't been together long, certainly not long enough for the girls in the high school to respect any relationship boundaries that weren't set in stone yet. Julie Monroe stepped right in and began flirting with Rick, who seemed to eat it up. By the way, what is it with you men and your egos? A pretty girl bats her eyes at you and you lose all your senses."

"She said parenthetically." Brad tugged on his cap.

"Well, it's true."

"What can I say?" He smirked.

"Anyway, desperate times call for drastic measures. I was already pretty good with my guitar, so I wrote him a love song and talked the powers that be into allowing me to perform it over the school's PA system one morning after the announcements. It was close to Valentine's Day, so they let me get away with it. I dedicated it to him. It caused quite a stir among the students. Some praised me for my song, some praised me for my courage, and a few mocked or teased me. But Rick pulled me aside after first period and apologized for the way he'd been acting. That's when I realized the power of music."

"And is that when you decided to become a musician?" Brad said.

"No follow-up questions—especially since this is a bonus round." She smiled so Brad would know she was just kidding. Sort of.

* * *

Everybody seemed content for a moment to take in the winter wonderland through the window. Ray got up to add a couple of more logs to the fire and it roared back to life.

Brad couldn't remember a Christmas like this one. His parents went all out for the holidays when he was young, but he was more focused on baseball than the festivities, which made him an oddball among his friends. While they were busy talking about what they were going to get for Christmas, he was at the indoor batting cages down the street all winter working on his swing.

After he got married and had children, Christmas ended up

being more about logistics—running from one relative's house to the next and attending Christmas parties, which meant they were rarely home to celebrate it. And wherever they ended up celebrating, it was often a blur of activity. They rarely just sat and talked for any length of time.

Ray shuffled over to the television. "Before we begin round two, let's see if we can find a weather update on TV." He glanced up at the clock on the wall. "The news will be on at noon—in just a few minutes."

Sarah stretched, waking Snowball from his slumber. He meowed in protest, stood on Sarah's lap, and went through his own stretching routine. Then he scampered toward the Christmas tree and curled up underneath. Once he got up, everybody followed suit.

Alma came around with a plate of cookies. How could Brad refuse? He took a couple of the chocolate chip variety and one peanut butter.

Sarah refused the plate—apparently she had will power.
Unlike me.

Brad glanced her way and they made eye contact. "So, were you avoiding my question about the moment you knew you wanted to become a recording artist someday because the answer is none of my business?"

She shook her head. "It's complicated. In a way, that was the defining moment, but in my day, we had more time to dream. Not as many teens chased careers in Nashville, partly because most parents couldn't afford to do such a thing and partly because it just wasn't the way it was done. The prevailing thought was, you had to pay your dues first—even though a few singers did hit it big early in the generation before me, but it didn't happen nearly as often as it does today.

63

"I never thought of that, but you're right. How old was Taylor Swift when she hit it big—seventeen?"

Sarah nodded. "I think so."

"And didn't her parents move her to Nashville when she was like fourteen, hoping she would get a record deal?" He finished off the last of his peanut butter cookie and set his sights on the remaining chocolate chip cookies.

Sarah nodded. "She was just following in the footsteps of LeAnn Rimes, Meghan Andrews, and others. But the process has been sped up even more by reality television. So many music shows focus on young talent, now. Miranda Lambert was discovered on *Nashville Star*. Carrie Underwood hit it big on *American Idol*. Cassadee Pope and Danielle Bradbery found success after winning *The Voice*. Then Lifetime Channel developed a show called *Chasing Nashville* that featured young teens chasing their dreams of becoming a country music superstar. It's never-ending now, it seems."

Was that a hint of cynicism he detected? After being a bit guarded to start with, she was beginning to open up. The more he got to know about her, the less she seemed like the performer he always admired from afar and the more she seemed like a real person. "Are you happy that such television programs weren't around when you were coming up?"

Snowball pranced up behind Sarah and began doing figure eights between her legs, catching her off guard again. "Ohhh."

"He likes you."

She reached down and scratched him on top of his head. He must have liked it because he flipped onto his back and purred. Sarah bent down and scratched him under the neck. Snowball began jerking his legs in all directions in a seemingly uncontrollable display of pure joy. "I like cats, but I've never owned one as an adult. I don't know what he sees in me."

Compassion, attentiveness, and maybe a tad bit of heartache. "Maybe he's just a good judge of character."

"Aw, that's sweet. So, tell me more about your ki—"

Ray shushed them. The news was starting.

A well-groomed man in his late twenties smiled at the camera from behind the desk. "I'm Greg Walker. Thanks for being with us. The weather is our top story today here on KKTV, Channel 11. Snow totals in southern Colorado are much higher than originally expected. Let's go over to Jack for the details."

The camera panned over to a man who was probably in his late forties. "A low-pressure system dropped farther south than our models were showing and that system collided with the warm air coming up from New Mexico." Jack pointed to the low-pressure system on the map and lifted both hands above his head with his palms up to create a visual for the rising warm air. His sleeves were rolled up. He'd probably been at the station for many hours tracking the storm.

"We already have fourteen inches of snow on the ground and could see as much as eight to ten more from another storm that has formed behind the first one," he continued. "The first storm began tapering off overnight and we've just about seen the end of it. The second storm should arrive this afternoon and continue into the evening, if our models hold up."

The camera returned to Greg. "Electrical outages are possible. Interstate 25, south of Walsenburg, is closed to the border. So are all of the major highways south of Walsenburg—none of which are expected to reopen until after Christmas Day. Road crews have been busy, but they have been unable to keep up. I-25 is their priority right now. Let's go out to KKTV reporter Dan West, who is reporting live from I-25, near Walsenburg."

Brad hated that he wasn't going to be with his kids for Christmas. But if he had to be stuck somewhere for the holidays, he certainly didn't mind being stranded with Sarah Rose.

Chapter 10

Megan watched Brad and Sarah from afar. Sarah was standing in front of Brad and leaning in slightly—a sure sign that she was into him. Megan hadn't seen that coming. Feeling like a third wheel, she contemplated going back to her room. Why was it so easy for some people to make a human connection and so difficult for her? Snowball trotted toward her, leaped onto the chair next to Megan, and butted his head again her thigh.

"You sure are a cute little thing." She stroked his back and patted him on his bottom a couple of times.

"Meooooowwwwww." He rolled over so she could scratch his belly, nearly falling off the chair.

Ray approached her. "Looks like Snowball is going to be a two-cat person this Christmas. That's unusual for him." He reached down and rubbed Snowball's belly. "Hey, if you need to go back to your room for a while, I'll clear the path for you."

"I hate to keep asking you to do it, but I feel like I need to freshen up and make a few calls."

"You're our guest. I'll be happy to do it anytime."

While Ray shoveled, Megan grabbed a few snacks and a bottle of water to take to her cabin, planning to skip lunch at the lodge. Thirty minutes later, she was video chatting with Rebecca.

"Take me on a tour of your cabin," Rebecca said.

Megan put the computer on her lap with the camera facing outward and began the tour. "Check out this bed—love the huge wooden posts."

"Niiiiiiiice."

"And what I wouldn't give to own a vanity like this." She stopped for a minute so Rebecca could get a good look. "It would take up half my room back in Omaha. I have the smallest bedroom out of the four girls who live there because I signed up last."

"My grandmother used to have one like that," Rebecca said. "She called it a 'bureau.' She would sit me on her lap when I was little and brush my hair. I loved the huge mirror and the sight of her brushing my hair. Made me feel so loved. I'd forgotten all about that."

Megan winced, trying to recall a time when her grandmother had brushed her hair like that, but she couldn't think of a single instance. Her grandmother just wasn't the type. She was strong and steady, always there when Megan needed her, but tenderness wasn't her strongest characteristic.

"I want to see the snow."

"It's freezing outside, girl. You'll have to settle for seeing it through the window." Megan wheeled herself over and lifted the laptop so Rebecca could get a peek.

"Whoa, I can see the path you've been talking about. If you get another ten inches, the piles on the sides of the path will be higher than you are. Cool."

"I don't know how cool it is, but there's nothing I can do to change it." Megan finished the tour by showing Rebecca the kitchen, entertainment center, and the small table and chairs in the corner. Alma would probably be calling soon to try to convince her to come back to the lodge for lunch, but she really just wanted to relax. She spun the laptop back around so she could see Rebecca.

"How's everything going there?"

"Besides being stuck here through Christmas Day?" Megan rolled her eyes and considered her next words. "I haven't told you this, but money is tight." She broke eye contact with Rebecca. "After shelling out money I didn't plan to spend for two or three nights here, I don't see how I'll be able to come and see you for a late Christmas."

Rebecca's eyes got big. "Oh, you're coming. Expenses are not an issue. I'll cover them. I really need to see you. It's been way too long."

"But—"

"But nothing. I got this."

Tears formed in Megan's eyes. "I feel like I've been trying so hard, but I can't make ends meet on a part-time barista's salary, even though I'm sharing expenses with three other students."

"I bet most of the students at Creighton, including your roommates, are getting some sort of help from their parents. You are completely alone. I have no idea how you've done it this far."

Megan picked up her cell phone and flipped through some photos, finally stopping on the one she was looking for. "I had plenty of help." She showed her a picture of her grand-parents who were posing with Rebecca and Megan at Megan's fourteenth birthday party.

"I haven't seen that picture in forever!" Rebecca said. That sure brings back memories." Her eyes got big again. "Hey, I was planning to hit you with this when you got here, but I need an assistant to help around here and I've been thinking about hiring somebody. You would be perfect. I know you, I trust you, and I could pay you more than you are making at the coffee shop."

"But I'm in school ..."

"I've been doing a little research and Penn Foster here in town offers a dental assistant certification." Rebecca tilted her head and put her hands in the air. "You've been going back and forth between becoming a dental assistant or a dental hygienist anyway. Penn Foster probably isn't as prestigious as Creighton, but who cares? You can earn a certificate there while you work for me. What do you say?"

It sounded perfect. "Are you for real?"

"Absolutely."

"I'll have to think about it."

After hanging up, she called Alma, telling her she had plenty to snack on until dinner time so she was just going to relax until then. Alma took the news better than she expected, which made Megan suspicious.

* * *

Do you want to go for a walk?" Brad said.

"In this?" Sarah pointed out the window.

"We might not get far, but it could be fun. I'm going a little stir crazy."

"So you're the rugged outdoors type, huh?" *Sarah Rose. Did you just flirt? When is the last time you did that?*

"I won't claim to be rugged, but I do love the outdoors. You in?"

Her eyes darted toward the window and then back to Brad. *Why not?* She nodded. As she was slipping on her coat, she noticed Alma jab Ray in the ribs with her elbow.

"We'll be back in thirty minutes or so," Brad said. "We're just going to get some air."

Ray and Alma smiled, nodding once.

Sarah shivered when they stepped outside. The snow had finally stopped, at least for a while. "Tell me more about your kids."

Brad led them down the freshly shoveled path toward Megan's cabin. The path was barely wide enough for two people to fit side by side, so they touched shoulders as they walked. The snow and leaves crunched under their feet.

"Ryan is twenty and he's known what he wanted to do since he was seven," Brad said. "He's a sophomore at the University of Denver where he's studying graphic design. He wants to design websites, logos, and signage. He already knows how to do all that, and has been doing it for quite some time—at least as far as websites and logos are concerned, but he knew a degree would lead to a better paying job."

"Smart boy," Sarah said. "What's his personality like?"

"Outgoing, confident, compassionate. He's just well-grounded. That had much more to do with his mother than me."

Sarah tugged her wool cap lower to cover her ears. "It's good to hear you speak highly of her, even though you're no longer together."

They reached Megan's cabin and Brad directed Sarah behind it by touching her back.

"Where in the world are you taking me? And do you realize I'm wearing sneakers? It's a good thing I didn't wear my loafers." Sarah plunged one foot into the snow before he answered. And then another. She imagined she looked like she was walking in quicksand.

Brad raised his arm and pointed. "If we can just get to that tree line, the snow shouldn't be quite so deep. In fact, look." He pointed toward a strip of grass that followed the tree line. Apparently, the trees had blocked the snow.

Ten minutes later, they reached the tree line and stomped the snow off their shoes as best they could.

Sarah could just hear her mother now. "What kind of man takes a woman in sneakers on a walk after a snowstorm?" She had to admit, taking a long romantic walk in the snow looked far more romantic in the movies.

They had natural chemistry. She couldn't deny that. She couldn't remember the last time she allowed a man to lead her anywhere, much less took a walk in the woods with one.

"How about your daughter? What's her story?"

"Amy is nineteen. She's always been into theater. When she was little, she would dress up and act out parts from movies in front of our family. She's taken a few acting classes here and there, but school really doesn't appear to be her thing, and she's finding out that she prefers to work behind the curtain. She found a job on a prep crew at a community theater in Albuquerque."

"It sounds like she's figuring things out," Sarah said.

"I think so. She has a roommate, picks up other odd jobs here and there, and is working her way up the ladder. She really does seem happy. I just hate to see her struggle, but I understand chasing a passion."

Sarah nodded. "What's she like?"

"Thoughtful and intelligent with a fierce independent streak.

72

She'll always be my little girl, though, no matter how independent she might be."

"Spoken like a true father." Sarah paused. "Do you mind me asking why you and Karen split?"

Brad touched her back again, directing her eastward. "It's complicated, but isn't that always the case?"

"If you don't want to get into it—"

"It's not that. I'm just embarrassed. I was mostly to blame—too much time chasing a dream that never came to fruition and too little time at home. When I played high school baseball, Karen was fine with it. And she supported my early attempts to work my way up to the big leagues after I signed with the Phillies. But after Ryan and Amy arrived, she eventually got tired of parenting alone and planning our lives around the off-season."

In the distance, they saw a squirrel's tail sticking up out of the snow. Apparently, he was digging for food. They stopped for a minute to watch him.

"Everybody in the game—broadcasters, scouts, coaches, players—gets married in the off-season," Brad said, picking up where he left off. "And they go on family vacations in the off-season. So everything has to happen in October, November, or December, assuming your team doesn't make the playoffs, and assuming you don't get sent to fall or winter ball."

"Seems like a lot to ask of a person," Sarah said.

"For the family or the player?"

"Both, I guess. But I do admire your tenacity. Nobody ever achieved a dream without hardship."

They walked on in silence.

Brad glanced down, clearly feeling remorse for choosing his career over his family, but life was rarely that simple. Family should come first, but a career is necessary and sometimes a career takes you away from your family for periods of time. She understood that better than anybody.

Even so, she had to ask the question. "So ... she left you?"

He didn't answer right away, but eventually, he nodded. "She found someone else."

"Ouch."

They strolled past the squirrel, who was still too busy looking for food to even notice them. For the first time, she noticed the gurgling noise of the river.

"She was my first love, which made it even harder for me to get over her," Brad said. "After our divorce, I had a nagging sense that I might love another someday, but I was afraid it wouldn't be with the same intensity."

She knew what that felt like. "Hmm."

"I didn't mean to bring up bad memories for you. I've read enough of your interviews over the years to know that Rick was your first love."

A man who can read a woman's "hmm" is rare. It's even more rare for a relative stranger. But he does have the advantage of knowing about my personal life. "Second love doesn't sound nearly as sexy, does it?"

Brad laughed. "Never heard it put that way, but no, it really doesn't."

They walked on in silence for a few more minutes before Brad suggested they turn around and head back, saying he didn't want to worry Ray and Alma.

A few flakes began to fall again during their walk back to the lodge. Sarah stuck out her tongue, trying to catch them and she felt Brad's eyes on her as she did so, causing a stir in her stomach.

Chapter 11

The silence between Brad and Sarah on their way back to the lodge was comfortable. Brad had this theory about silence in a relationship. If two people were comfortable enough around each other to not feel like they had to say something to fill the dead air, then they had something special. He was far from being in a relationship with Sarah, but the brief time he spent with her awoke something inside him that had been dormant for far too long.

Brad considered knocking on Megan's door when they passed her cabin but thought better of it. She had made her feelings about him known. No reason to press the issue. But he really did feel for her, especially after learning she had been bullied in school. The mere thought angered him. Life was hard enough without having to deal with people who want to tear a person down simply because she was physically challenged. He hoped he would get another shot at knowing Megan before they all went their separate ways. He sensed there was more to her story.

"I'm going to stop by my cabin for a few minutes to freshen up and make a phone call or two," Sarah said. "I'll meet you back at the lodge after bit."

"Sure thing."

They lingered before she finally broke away and headed for her cabin.

* * *

Abigail's face appeared on Sarah's computer screen. "Are you doing alright, honey? You look a little flushed."

"I just got back from a walk," Sarah said.

"A walk? What in the world? You'll catch get your death of a cold out there, girl. What's wrong with you?" Abigail stroked Espresso's fur. She was curled up in Abigail's lap.

"I'll be fine, Mom. I went with somebody."

"A stranger?"

"Oh, I can't win."

"Was this stranger a man?" Abigail bit her lower lip, as if she were trying to contain a smile.

"He's just Brad—one of the residents who is stranded here too. By the way, it is official. The roads will be closed through Christmas Day. So I'll see you the day after Christmas, okay?"

"Sounds like somebody is changing the subject."

"You're impossible, Mom."

* * *

After calling Ray to let him know they would be back over soon, Brad called Ryan. As much as he enjoyed FaceTiming with his kids, he always felt awkward when he held the camera on his

76

end—often cutting off half his own head. So, he usually opted for an old-fashioned phone call.

"Has there been any change in the weather, Dad?"

"It's actually worse than they predicted. I'll be stuck here through Christmas Day. Maybe we can do a late Christmas on the 26th or 27th—whenever I can get there? You'll still be on a winter break from school, won't you?"

"I'm off until after the first week in January. A late Christmas works for me. A friend invited me to his family's Christmas celebration, so I might take him up on it."

"What about Amy?"

"She flew in this morning and has already settled into her hotel room, not far from my campus. I'll take care of her. And she's welcome to come with me to my friend's place. Her theater is shut down until January for the holidays, so I don't think she'll mind sticking around for an extra day or two, but you should check with her."

"Thanks for the update. I'll check on her after we hang up."

"You seem different ... in a good way."

Brad took a seat in a brown easy chair. "How so?"

"Like you're less burdened or something, or at least, not as sad. Your tone is different."

"Good to hear."

"So what's going on?"

"Can I get back to you on that? Might be a tad bit early to say anything."

Ryan let him off the hook.

Brad told him he would call him in the next day or two to figure out their plans. "Merry Christmas, son."

"Merry Christmas to you too, Dad."

Brad dialed Amy's number, but her phone went to voice mail.

He left her a message explaining his situation, saying he would touch base with her again soon.

After hanging up, he had the strangest feeling wash over him. He spent most of his life in various rundown hotels and motels all across the country and they always provided adequate shelter from the demands of the outside world. In fact, he usually couldn't wait to close the door and slide the chain on the lock because it meant he was on his own for the next eight hours. But right now, all he could think about was what Sarah was doing in the cabin next door.

He pushed himself out of his chair and looked out the window toward Sarah's cabin. He thought he caught a glimpse of her looking toward his cabin, but she was gone so fast that he couldn't be certain. *Maybe she was just checking to see if the snow was picking up again.*

A deer scampered between their cabins. Two more followed. It really was a scene that could have appeared on a Christmas card. He grabbed his camera and began shooting pictures through the window. He rarely talked about his photography hobby because he didn't think he was very good, but that didn't stop him from shooting nearly everywhere he went. He had photos of every ballpark he had ever played or coached in. He also had thousands of photos of teammates, coaches, and managers he had taken over the years.

As much joy as the photos brought him, his photography also reminded him about the time he spent away from his family. Large gaps in the photos of Ryan and Amy—most of which were taken during the off-season—meant their appearance had changed drastically from one set of photos to the next. He wished he could turn back the clock. He would handle so many things differently.

He eased the front door open and crept around the corner of his cabin so he could get a clear view of the deer. He squatted and shot a dozen or more photos. Their ears perked up at his presence and eventually, they took off. Brad shot a photo of Sarah's cabin and one of his own.

He glanced back at her cabin. The pull was just too much to resist. He approached her door and knocked. She answered, waving him inside.

* * *

Megan awoke from her nap and stretched. The leather couch was as comfortable as her bed, especially after she started a fire in the fireplace and then curled up under her comforter. She had been hoping to catch a Christmas movie on the Hallmark Channel, but she dozed off as soon as her head hit the pillow, sleeping for nearly two hours. Thinking she could still catch one of those movies, she flipped through the stations, trying to find the channel.

A Christmas Wish was just starting. It was one of Megan's favorites—about a mother named Martha and her children who are on the verge of being homeless when they move to another town in a last-ditch effort to make a new life. They find themselves at the mercy of strangers—one of whom is the owner of a diner, who gives her a job. As she gets to know some of the locals, they devise a plan to make it Martha's best Christmas yet.

The idea of being at the mercy of strangers scared Megan to death, but yet, here she was, about to spend the holidays with four strangers. She couldn't help but note that she had already received more compassion and acceptance here than she had in most other places she had frequented in her life.

Alma told her when she checked in that her cupboards contained snack food, so she got up to see if that included popcorn, because what's a movie without popcorn? As she was rolling toward the kitchen, the lights flickered twice, and then went off. "That's just great."

Alma called Megan's cell phone. "This happens in the mountains sometimes, dear. Ray has a small gas generator for such emergencies and he's getting her cranked up right now. Unfortunately, it doesn't provide enough power for the entire facility, but it'll provide enough for the lodge for a while."

"So we're going to have to sleep in the lodge?"

"Hard to say, but we're preparing for the possibility of no power for a while. Crews won't even be able to get here for a couple of days since the highway is closed."

"That's just great."

"We'll take good care of you, dear."

Brad and Sarah passed by her front window and knocked on her door. A cold blast of air stung her face when she answered. And, unbelievably, it was starting to snow again.

"Ready to head back to the lodge?" Sarah asked.

"I'll freeze to death if I stay in here. Let me get my coat. Come on in."

They stepped inside.

"These cabins are something else, aren't they?" Sarah brushed a little snow off her jacket and took it all in. "This one is structured a little differently than mine. I love the little breakfast nook you have over in the corner. Apparently, each one has its own unique design."

Megan scooted forward in her wheelchair and slipped her coat on. "Yeah, this is a pretty cool place—except for losing power just now. Apparently, that's a thing here. Alma says it could come and go for the next couple of days. Ray has a gas generator, but it sounds like it is pretty limited."

"We've got a fireplace back at the lodge with plenty of wood to keep us warm," Brad said. "I think Alma has the food situation figured out. We'll be fine. We'll just have to count on each other a little more."

Yeah, that's one of the many problems I have with this little situation. Megan pulled her cap down over her ears and wrapped her scarf around her face. "Okay, ready as I'm going to be."

Brad pushed Megan's wheelchair through the snow, raising the front wheels so they didn't get bogged down, while Sarah followed them. Halfway to the lodge, they bumped into Ray who was just beginning to clear the path again.

"Hey, don't worry about it, Ray," Brad said. "We can manage."

Creeper dude wasn't such a creeper anymore. His attention was clearly focused on Sarah, and he really did seem to be a good guy. But seeing Brad and Sarah on the way to coupledom made her feel like a fifth wheel. Maybe she was just looking for an excuse to feel alienated. It wouldn't be the first time.

A warm blast of air swept over her when they entered the lodge. How long would the generator keep the heat on? The lights were dimmer, but the fireplace was roaring—at least they would always have the fireplace. Megan thought she detected a hint of cinnamon in the air.

"Perfect timing," Alma said. "I just made some hot cocoa with my secret ingredient.

Ray took their coats and rolled his eyes. "She thinks cinnamon is a secret ingredient."

She stomped her foot in mock protest. "Well, it isn't any-more."

Everyone gravitated toward the nook, taking a seat around the same table—the one closest to the window so they could get the best view of the snow, which continued to fall. Alma set coffee mugs in front of each person and filled them with her hot cocoa, except Brad, who passed.

Ray was the last one to take a seat. "I have good news and bad news."

"I feel like I need to hear the good news first," Megan said.

"The small gas generator I have can last five hours on a tank of propane, maybe longer if we go into conservation mode."

"And the bad news?" Sarah said.

"We only have two tanks of gas."

Chapter 12

"When you say 'conservation mode,' what does that look like in practical terms?" Brad tugged on his baseball cap.

"Well, of course, there's no way of knowing how long this outage will last, but just to be safe we'll need to keep lamps turned off, unless we really need them," Ray said. "The darker, the better, except for the firelight. We do have plenty of firewood to get us through. I'm really hoping to keep the refrigerator on the grid, but there may come a time when we have to unplug it too. I've already gone around and unplugged every other appliance. The only one I didn't budge on was the coffee pot." He grinned.

"How often does this happen?" Sarah bit her lower lip.

"Several times a year," Ray said. "But it's usually for short periods of time. We've only gone without electricity for more than one day on one occasion. That's when I decided to get the generator. Oh, and I should mention that the furnace won't work if we run out of gas in the generator because the furnace requires electricity, so the fireplace would be our primary source of heat."

"We can make do. It might even be fun." The aroma of the hot cocoa tickled Sarah's nostrils. "Oh, this smells heavenly."

Alma took a seat at their table. "Thank you, but before you get too adventurous, one of the compromises we'll need to make is Christmas Eve dinner. I intended to go all out, but I'm afraid we'll need to scale back a bit."

"Would anybody object to an indoor weenie roast over the fire?" Ray asked. "It'll allow us to keep the oven off."

"Sounds perfect," Brad said.

"At least you'll have a great story to tell later." Alma pushed herself up from the table. "Ray already went out and collected a few sticks we can use to cook them." She picked them up from the counter and distributed them.

Sarah excused herself to help Alma in the kitchen with the side dishes, giving Brad a chance to talk to Megan, who was sitting across from him, but when Sarah left, Megan rolled over to the coffee pot, saying she wanted more hot cocoa. He wondered if she would return to the same table.

Megan set her nearly full mug between her knees and pushed her way back to the table. Clearly, she could take care of herself.

Brad changed his mind about the hot cocoa—partially because he needed a distraction and partially because it smelled so good. He got up to pour himself a mug full. "Hope you got a little rest this afternoon," he said over his shoulder.

"I got a nap in, but I was hoping to catch a Christmas movie—one of my favorites was just about to start when the power went off."

Brad returned to the table. "Are you a movie buff?"

"Totally. And I'm a sucker for sappy Christmas movies. The sappier the better. How about you? Are you into movies?"

"I enjoy them sometimes, but I'm more of a reader. I spend my life in motels. Games often get over late and I really look forward to crawling into bed with a good book for an hour or so before I drift off to sleep."

"I wouldn't have figured you for a reader. You don't really look like one."

He smiled. "What exactly does a reader look like?"

"Good point. What do you like to read?"

"I've read everything Richard Ford has ever written. John Grisham too. But I'll also pick up the occasional non-fiction book. I just finished reading the Steve Jobs biography. And *The Bullpen Gospels* is a must-read for every minor leaguer. Read that not long ago too." He took a big swig from his mug and made a contorted face.

Megan laughed. "Not what you were expecting?"

"It's so sweet. Ugh." He paused for a second, setting his mug down. "Can I ask you a serious question?"

"I guess."

"Did the bullying stop after high school? You aren't still bullied in college, are you?"

"Mean girls exist everywhere in society, but they can't get away with it as much after high school. So it's more subtle now."

Brad made eye contact. "How so?"

"They whisper, roll their eyes ..."

"Who are 'they,' if you don't mind me asking?"

"People at school, in grocery stores, coffee shops—anywhere people gather. The funny thing is, though, it always happens in groups. Mob rule, I guess." She sighed and stared into her hot cocoa. "Some probably wouldn't call it bullying after high school, but being belittled still feels like bullying to me."

Her eyes narrowed ever so slightly, allowing Brad to recognize her pain. Brad had seen bullying during his days as a player—the locker room could be a vicious place. Players called it hazing, saying it was all in good fun, but it wounded some players, causing them to withdraw. He had stood up to more than one locker room bully in his day. Now he wished he could do it again for Megan.

* * *

Sarah returned to the room to see Brad and Megan deep in conversation. She gave them their space when she heard what they were discussing. Brad was obviously trying to get to know Megan better, and Sarah was moved by the small portion of the conversation she did overhear.

Ray pushed the front door open, stomped off his boots, and removed his hat. "Looks like we are on the verge of overloading the generator. It keeps sputtering. We're going to have to cut back on even more luxuries—no more television. I'm going to search for my old transistor radio since it runs on batteries."

"This could get interesting," Sarah said.

Ray unplugged everything except the refrigerator and the coffee pot, and headed into the private living quarters, saying he was going to find some candles.

Alma came out of the kitchen with a plate full of uncooked hot dogs and set them on the coffee table in the den. She returned to the kitchen and came back out with a large container of potato salad, a bag of potato chips, and a couple of packages of hot dog buns. "Who wants to go first?"

"I think Brad should be the guinea pig," Sarah said. "Once he burns his first attempt, then the rest of us will know how close to the fire we should get."

"Thanks for the vote of confidence." Brad grabbed one of the sharpened sticks Ray had gathered from outside and pierced a hot dog. He jabbed it into the fireplace, and when he realized he was a little too close to the fire, he raised it a few inches. Within seconds, juices began flowing out of it, dripping into the fire, making a hissing noise each time one hit the flame.

"Not bad." Sarah punched him on the arm in a playful manner.

"Thanks ... I think," he said.

A few minutes later, Ray re-entered the room with a radio and several candles, setting everything on the coffee table near the fireplace. He spaced the candles out on opposite ends and lit them, giving the living room a campfire look and feel.

Alma flipped the radio on. Mariah Carey's version of "Hark! The Herald Angels Sing" began to play. Alma turned it up and hummed along.

Brad finished cooking the first hot dog and pulled it off the stick to examine it. "Okay, so maybe it *is* a little too well done." He showed Sarah the end he burned.

"A little?" Sarah said.

"Cut a ballplayer some slack. We aren't all that accustomed to cooking." He pointed toward Megan. "It's your turn. Grab a stick—in fact, we can all fit in front of the fire." Brad made some extra room for Megan.

Sarah took note of his thoughtfulness. *How is this guy not married?*

Sarah and Megan shoved their hot dogs over the fire, twisting them to make sure the heat was evenly distributed. If the truth were to be told, Sarah suspected both she and Megan were going for perfection their first time out to show up Brad. Their efforts didn't produce perfection, but their hot dogs looked considerably better than Brad's first effort.

"This is what it's supposed to look like." Megan pointed at her masterpiece.

"Yeah, yeah," Brad said.

A few minutes later, they settled into their familiar places in the den. Sarah didn't know how the others felt, but to her, the five of them already felt like old friends. *We didn't even know each other twenty-four hours ago.*

"This next song is from Lady Antebellum's Christmas album called *On This Winter's Night.* Here is "The First Noel.""

"Oh, I love this song!" Sarah's eyes got wide. "Mom used to play this on the piano every Christmas and we would sing along. Dad had a horrible voice, but that didn't stop him from singing too."

"Are your parents still alive?" Brad took a bite of his hot dog and set it back down on his plate.

"I was on my way to see Mom yesterday. She's still doing well. Dad passed away a few years ago."

"I'm sorry."

"He was ready to go after a long bout with prostate cancer."

Ray and Alma finished preparing their food and took a seat.

"Everyone up for picking up where we left off with our index cards?" Ray said.

"Let's do it." Sarah really wanted to hear more from Brad. He almost sounded too good to be true. But she was also interested in hearing more about Megan. She felt a strong connection with her.

"We worked our way around the room once, so we're back to Megan," Alma said.

Megan let out a mock evil laugh. "I have all the power!"

"Somebody's really getting into this," Brad said.

"I choose Brad this time." Megan flipped over her next card. "What is your favorite photo and why?"

Chapter 13

"My dad was a coal miner back in Farmington." Brad took another bite of his hot dog. "It was a good living, but my sister and I rarely saw him. But he always found a way to take my sister and me to the Connie Mack World Series every summer. It's a well-known tournament held at Ricketts Park for youth and it's a big deal to play in it." He paused to take a drink of water.

"As fun as it was for all of us to go as a family every year, it was even more fun when I got to play in it during my sophomore year in high school. The families get to go down on the field for pre-game ceremonies. Someone snapped a photo of my family and me near home plate. Dad ... he died in the mines a couple of weeks later."

He reached into his back pocket, pulled out his billfold, and removed the photo. He glanced at it before passing it around the room. "This is a smaller version than the one I have framed in my office. It represents the last innocent year of my life. Everything changed after that."

"Is your mom still alive?" Sarah asked.

"After losing Dad, something broke inside her. Her personality changed from happy, outgoing, and happy-go-lucky, to withdrawn, introverted, and depressed. My younger sister,

Denise, and I would come home from school and have to walk on eggshells. We never knew when she was going to snap. She never harmed us. But she drank too much and yelled a lot. One day, a month or two after Dad died, Denise and I came home from school and my Aunt Julie was there."

Megan pursed her lips. *I completely misjudged this dude. He had his own difficulties growing up.* "What happened to your mom?"

"Denise and I went to live with Aunt Julie. She would only say Mom was gone because she needed to get some help. Aunt Julie never married, so it was a real adjustment for her to have two teenagers in her house all of a sudden."

Sarah shook her head, seeming to be in disbelief. "Are you in contact with your mother now?"

"She never came back and I never reached out. Eventually, she severed all ties with Aunt Julie. I was always too poor to hire a PI to try to find her—even after I began my pro career. Most minor leaguers live like paupers. I was no exception.

"As I got older and had the means to try to track her down, I never could bring myself to do it." He set his plate on the couch next to him and wiped his mouth with a napkin. "What if I found her, against her wishes, and she told me she simply didn't want to have anything to do with Denise or me? I couldn't take that. I would rather live with the illusion that maybe she had some other reason—one that wasn't so cruel."

"Have you ever Googled her name?" Megan said.

"I rarely think about her anymore. It's just easier that way."

He didn't really answer the question, but Megan certainly wasn't going to press the issue.

The DJ interrupted. "This next song is a Kelly Clarkson tune called 'Underneath the Tree,' by request, from her Christmas album called 'Wrapped in Red.' I hope you have somebody waiting for you under the mistletoe who is wrapped in red this holiday season.

Ugh.

Megan hated being single, especially at the holidays, but it was better than being with Tim—the guy she broke up with recently after hanging out with him for over a year. He turned out to be everything Rebecca warned her about. He had a wandering eye. And he was always on her case to lose a few pounds. She wasn't overweight, but even if she were, that would have gotten old really fast.

Megan never had any problem attracting guys, but once in a while, men would act awkward around her—apparently, wondering how they would handle somebody in a wheelchair. But she always tried to put their minds at ease as quickly as possible by showing her self-sufficiency. That's why she usually drove herself to coffee shops or restaurants when a guy asked her out. She had a point to prove.

She'd only had one serious boyfriend in her life: Tim. But shortly after they split up, her inheritance ran out. Lonely and struggling, every whisper or finger point was more noticeable as she did her grocery shopping or as she was filling her car with gas.

She was growing bitter again—a demon she thought she conquered shortly after graduating from high school. That's the main reason she was headed to Chama to visit Rebecca. She needed to be around somebody who loved her—somebody who could help her get back on track.

And she had to admit, she had been thinking about Rebecca's offer. She had nothing tying her to Omaha any longer.

* * *

"My turn, right?" Sarah looked each person in the eye. "I choose Megan." She flipped her next card over. "What is the craziest belief or conspiracy theory that one of your family members can't stop talking about?"

Megan looked toward the ceiling, contemplating her answer. "Can't say my grandparents had any crazy beliefs, but I had an uncle who believed the government was hiding aliens in Hangar 18 on some air force base in Ohio after they crashed in the 1940s or '50s." She shrugged. "I don't remember the details, but I do remember him believing it and I feel like he tried to get everybody else to believe it too."

Brad shook his head. "How does a person fall for something like that?"

"He started connecting with other people on online forums who believed it as well," Megan said. "I didn't even want to have him anywhere near my friends because he would go on and on about it. It was embarrassing. But I didn't have to worry about that much. He didn't visit often."

"Up next," the DJ said, "is 'Do You Hear What I Hear?' by Jewell." Jewell was popular when Megan was small and she always loved her silky smooth voice. Releasing a new Christmas album was a brilliant move for her because her voice just sounded like Christmas.

"Brad, you're up next," Alma said.

Brad pointed toward Ray. "This one's for you." He flipped the card over. "How did you meet the love of your life?"

"Oh, good." Sarah rubbed her hands together. "Who doesn't like a good love story?"

Megan was anxious to hear the story too. What Ray and Alma had was special, which meant they were worth listening to. She certainly had a lot to learn when it came to picking men.

Ray made eye contact with Alma. "When I was a teenager, my family attended a Christmas Eve service at the Community Bible Church that used to be located just a few miles up the road." Ray pointed to his left. "Girls from the church sang a few traditional Christmas carols that night. I couldn't take my eyes off the girl in the middle of the back row."

Alma giggled.

"I was thirteen, she was fourteen," Ray said. "Later, I kidded her about having a thing for younger men. Eventually, I stopped doing that after she threatened to deck me." He chuckled. "Anyway, I approached her after the service and couldn't even look her in the eye, but I managed to say, ''You're pretty."

"He didn't even introduce himself." Alma waved her arms. "He just walks up, stares at the floor, and says, 'You're pretty.' By today's standards, that would be a little creepy, as kids would say."

"Well, I've never been all that hip."

"Hip?" Megan said.

"That's 1970s lingo for 'cool,' dear," Alma said.

"Lingo?" Megan laughed.

"Why didn't you two meet before that night?" Sarah said.

"Alma's family was new to the church," Ray said. "But I didn't waste any time in getting to know her. We've been together ever since."

* * *

Alma appreciated having a backstory to share with the inn's guests every year. The story was true. They were both assigned to the Christmas Eve service at Community Bible Church that night in 1946, although they never mentioned the year to the guests. Ray took on the appearance of a rather awkward teenage boy, and she was a giggly teenage girl who was allowed to join the choir at the last minute to sing several traditional Christmas carols.

Neither Ray nor Alma understood their full assignment at the time, but they were rarely given a lot of information up front. In fact, in her experience, angels worked on a need-to-know basis. The following Christmas, they were assigned as an elderly couple to run Mercy Inn. Neither had aged in appearance since. People seem to trust an elderly couple much more than they might trust a younger one—especially when it comes to opening up about matters of the heart. And Mercy Inn was all about matters of the heart.

* * *

The second storm moved in and the snow was falling heavily again, but Ray sensed less apprehension from the guests about being stranded. He got up and grabbed his black leather Bible off the bookshelf.

"Every Christmas Eve, we read the Christmas story from Luke 2." Ray took his seat. "Will it offend anybody if I do so again this year?"

Nobody objected. So he began.

In those days a decree went out from Caesar Augustus that all the world should be registered. This was the first registration when Quirinius was governor of Syria. And all went to be registered, each to his own town. And Joseph also went up from Galilee, from the town of Nazareth, to Judea, to the city of David, which is called Bethlehem, because he was of the house and lineage of David, to be registered with Mary, his betrothed, who was with child. And while they were there, the time came for her to give birth. And she gave birth to her firstborn son and wrapped him in swaddling cloths and laid him in a manger, because there was no place for them in the inn.

And in the same region there were shepherds out in the field, keeping watch over their flock by night. And an angel of the Lord appeared to them, and the glory of the Lord shone around them, and they were filled with great fear. And the angel said to them, "Fear not, for behold, I bring you good news of great joy that will be for all the people. For unto you is born this day in the city of David a Savior, who is Christ the Lord. And this will be a sign for you: you will find a baby wrapped in swaddling cloths and lying in a manger." And suddenly there was with the angel a multitude of the heavenly host praising God and saying, "Glory to God in the highest, and on earth peace among those with whom he is pleased!"

Ray closed his Bible. "Can you imagine what that must have looked like? Luke's account says there was a multitude of heavenly hosts praising God for this little one who would one day grow up the be the Savior of mankind."

Sarah nodded. "It's an incredible word picture. If I had been one of the shepherds, I would have been scared to death when the angel appeared—even though he said 'Fear not.'"

Ray's eyes softened. "A little healthy fear of the holy is a good thing, but the birth of Christ was a glorious event—it changed everything, giving mankind direct access to God for the first time, and he has been in the process of making all things new ever since. That means you can never find yourself in a circumstance he cannot redeem in some way. It's my belief that he even uses circumstances like snowstorms to quiet the noise in our lives long enough to do a redemptive work of some sort."

"That gives me goosebumps," Megan said.

"As well it should," Ray said. "God is with us."

Chapter 14

As the afternoon began to fade, Sarah had a perfect view of the snow from where she was sitting. It had drifted up to the base of a birdbath. Throw in the howling wind and she couldn't imagine Highway 17 being cleared tomorrow, even if the snow stopped by morning like the forecast said it would.

That wasn't such a bad thing. In the past twenty-four hours, she felt more alive than she had since Rick died. Not only was she smitten with Brad, but she had that old familiar stirring in her soul to write songs again. She had nearly forgotten what both felt like. But could Brad really fit into her life when they were going to be so far apart for so many months at a time?

If she did start writing songs again, she would record a new album and then go on tour, which could last as long as a year. And he would be on the road most of the year, traveling with his team. Maybe it would be better if this were just a Christmas romance and it ended here. It would be a great memory, but it wouldn't come with all of the potential difficulties.

"It looks like it's my turn, right?" Alma said.

Ray nodded.

Alma chose Sarah and flipped the next card. "What is your favorite book, and why?" She rubbed her hands together. "I always love this question. You can find out so much about people by what they read."

Sarah tucked a strand of hair behind her ear. "I read a memoir this summer called *Wild* by Cheryl Strayed that spoke to my soul. Are you all familiar with it?"

"I saw the movie with Reese Witherspoon, but never read the book," Megan said.

Brad shook his head.

"Strayed lost her mother to cancer at the age of twenty-two and her marriage died soon thereafter. A few years later, she made an impulsive decision to hike the Pacific Crest Trail from the Mohave Desert through California and Oregon all the way to Washington—eleven hundred miles in all. And she decided to do it alone, even though she had no previous hiking experience.

"She faced all sorts of trials—bears, snakes, ridiculously high temperatures, and record snowfalls. She pushed through the trials and it reoriented her life, healing her past hurts, and it helped her to begin living again." Sarah looked down at her feet.

"Weren't you twenty-two when you lost Rick?" Brad said.

She nodded. *Very perceptive.*

"So, in a way, after losing yourself for a number of years, you're standing on the starting line of your own Pacific Crest Trail," he said.

She turned to face him. "I'm not nearly as brave. In fact, I moved across the country so I could avoid the starting line and I've been avoiding it ever since."

"But yet, here you are ... standing on it right now," Brad said.

"I guess I just needed to be around people who care about who I am right now, not who I used to be." She fought back tears. "Spending Christmas with all of you has created a stir in me to begin writing again. But I'm terrified."

"What are the possible ramifications, dear?" Alma said.

"Writing songs leads to cutting an album. Cutting an album leads to interviews. Interviews lead to questions about why I disappeared from the music scene. And then there's the ensuing year-long tour. Fans will want to hear their favorite songs from my backlist. How can I stand onstage every night and sing about the man I loved and lost?"

Alma waited a few seconds before she said anything. When she finally spoke, Sarah saw kindness in her eyes. "This brings us back to the first question you answered this morning about using the gift God gave you for others. Honey, once you released those songs into the world, they no longer belonged to you. They belong to the teens who learned that true love is sacrificial by listening to your music. They belong to everybody who is on the verge of giving up on finding love, but are hanging on by a thread because they want what you and Rick had."

Sarah couldn't contain her tears any longer. She didn't even try. They burst from her eyes and rolled down her cheeks, performing a cleansing and healing work.

* * *

Alma wrapped her arms around Sarah.

Brad wasn't sure where he stood on the issue of music not belonging to the musician, but in a broader scope, he thought Alma probably had a point in the same way that during his playing days, the game featured entertainment and an escape for fans, while at the same time, the players were trying to advance their careers.

Regardless of where he stood on the issue, Sarah just had a breakthrough, and watching her physical reaction that resulted from the realization that she had been hiding since Rick's death put a knot in his stomach. He wished he were the one consoling her. Maybe it was too soon for that, but if he was reading all of the signs properly, she felt the same way about him as he did about her.

But if everything she just said about recording an album and then touring for a year was true, where did that leave them—especially if she moved back to Nashville while he worked nearly 800 miles away in Wilmington? It seemed too soon to be considering such things, but they only had one day left together. Once the highway was cleared and reopened, Sarah would be bound for Colorado Springs while he headed for Denver. At least they were headed in the same direction.

Maybe we could travel together? I could drop her off in Colorado Springs and I could head to Denver and then pick her up on the way back. Or, we could go to both places together. Since both Christmas celebrations would be late anyway, why not?

Sarah wiped her eyes and apologized.

"No need to apologize, dear." Alma stroked Sarah's hair. "This little game has led to many such cleansing tears. Contemplating the deeper things of life has a way of dredging up fears and wrong motives that really want to stay hidden. But when they are exposed to the light, they must flee."

Wrong motives. Brad had already confessed to Sarah he lost Karen, in large part, due to him chasing his dream at the expense of his marriage. He never had a good understanding of what balance looked like in this instance, but he already knew he wanted to show Sarah he was not willing to make the same mistake twice. He got up to refresh his coffee, mostly so he could give Alma and Sarah some space.

Megan wheeled herself toward the bathroom while Ray went to check on the generator. Ray had already informed everybody that once the first tank of gas ran out, he planned to keep the generator off until the next morning. He said the food would be fine in the refrigerator overnight, even though it wouldn't be plugged in.

Alma had already set out a number of finger foods for everybody to munch on throughout the evening and on into breakfast. They would have to make do without coffee in the morning, but that was the least of their concerns. Brad had lived on the road most of his professional life, so he was used to making adjustments on the fly.

Alma was now facing Sarah on the couch, holding her hands and looking into her eyes. Whatever she was saying, Sarah was taking it all in, nodding on occasion. Brad took a seat in the nook and stared out into the snow, making sure he could still see Alma and Sarah.

Creak.

The noise came from the den, directly over Alma and Sarah. They glanced up briefly but went right back to their discussion.

The lodge must be settling, probably as a result of the snow and changing temperatures.

Ray returned from checking on the generator, announcing that the first tank of gas was gone, so they were in rustic mode for the night. Brad watched him put a few cookies and chocolate-covered pretzels on a paper plate, then he took a seat at Brad's table.

"Does this place still settle sometimes?" Brad asked. "I just heard a creak from in there." He pointed toward the den.

"You know how it is with older places. Cracks appear in the wall out of nowhere. The ceiling and floorboards begin to creak."

"Very true."

Ray shoved one of his pretzels into his mouth and chewed it. "It's Christmas Eve night—what are some of your favorite Christmas Eve memories with your kids when they were growing up?" Ray said.

"When they were little, they couldn't wait to go to bed on Christmas Eve because they thought the sooner they went to bed, the sooner Santa would show up. After they got older, and life got more complicated and busy, Karen and I went for simplicity rather than magical and we began opening gifts on Christmas Eve night rather than the next morning."

Brad's eyes darted back and forth over Ray's shoulder to see how Sarah was doing. He still couldn't make out what Alma was saying to her, but Sarah was crying again. She was sitting cross-legged with her hands in her lap—the picture of vulnerability in Brad's mind.

"You would give anything to know what's going on over there, wouldn't you?" Ray winked.

"How about I plead the fifth and finish answering your first question instead?" Brad tugged on the bill of his cap.

Ray nodded, but he didn't even try to conceal his smirk.

"Karen would make a big juicy ham, a green bean casserole that couldn't be beat, a huge bowl of mashed potatoes, and a salad. She always had all sorts of desserts. Her pumpkin pie was my favorite. After stuffing ourselves, we would gather in the living room by the Christmas tree and open gifts."

"Did you and Karen visit her parents and your aunt with the kids on Christmas Day?"

"Most years, but all that running around made life pretty hectic."

Megan re-entered the room. "Mind if I join you?"

Ray waved her over. "The more the merrier."

She made a pit stop at the snack table, grabbing a few chocolate-covered pretzels and setting them on a paper plate on her lap.

Brad pulled a chair out so she could slide into the empty spot at the table.

"I have to stop eating all these sweets," she said.

"Easier said than done," Ray said.

Alma and Sarah appeared to be finished, so they joined the rest of the clan.

"So what's the plan for sleeping arrangements tonight?" Ray asked Alma.

"I was thinking you and I could stay out here with our special guests. Figured you and I could share a couch. Maybe Megan could take the other couch over in the corner. And I have a couple of air mattresses I'll set on the floor for Brad and Sarah. Does that work for everybody?"

Everybody nodded.

"I wouldn't mind if my mattress was close to the fireplace," Sarah said. "I can already feel a difference in the temperature." She shivered, running her hands up and down her arms.

"Will do." Alma went to fetch the air mattresses.

Ray followed her.

"This could be a little awkward," Megan said. "It sort of feels like the first night of camp with a bunch of strangers. You don't know what to expect, and as soon as you drift off to sleep, someone begins to snore."

"I should probably warn you—I have been told I sound like a

bear when I snore." Brad laughed. "I apologize in advance."

Megan rolled her eyes. "Great."

Chapter 15

Megan excused herself to call Rebecca. She rolled herself across the room and stopped near the front door, presumably to get a little privacy.

Sarah approached Brad in the nook, unable to conceal a slight frown. She couldn't help but wonder how Brad would view her outburst. Before that moment, she had the upper hand in the budding romance.

He was a diehard fan who fumbled for the right words when they first met, but something changed after that. He was slowly letting his guard down about his own failings and she had been accepting of him, which helped bolster his confidence. *Will he give me the same benefit of the doubt? No time like the present to find out.*

"You okay?" He motioned for her to take a seat.

She had to admit, it was a romantic setting. He had brought a candle back over from the coffee table in the living room and placed it on his table in the nook.

She sat down. "I'm embarrassed on a number of levels—first that I broke down like that in front of everybody, but then because I had never seen what Alma pointed out about my music not belonging to me."

He tugged on his baseball cap. "I have to confess ... I wonder about the validity of her statement."

Sarah pulled back slightly. "You do? I'm interested in hearing your take."

"Well ... my body of work took place on a baseball field. As a player, we entertained fans. I owed them my best effort, but after that, they went back to their lives and I went back to mine."

She nodded. "But I'm not sure it's the same thing. As musical artists, we create a product with the intention of people listening to it over and over. We give our own personal experiences a voice, knowing fans will understand what we are saying because they have gone through the same things."

Brad nodded and pursed his lips.

"We love to hear stories about the way our music helps someone through a rough patch. At one of my last concerts, a girl who was maybe fourteen scored a backstage pass by winning a radio contest. During the meet and greet, she asked me if she could talk to me about how one of my songs saved her life."

"Was she being overdramatic or was she being serious?"

"Either way, I wanted to hear her story."

"Now I want to hear it." He scooted his chair a little closer to the table and leaned in.

She smiled and wiped her eyes, just in case any tears remained. Her face felt puffy, which wasn't really the look she was going for with Brad, but she suspected they had already moved past looks. They had an undeniable spark. "I have a song called 'Stand Up.' Are you familiar with it?"

"It's an anthem about taking responsibility for your actions, right?"

She nodded. "So this girl—her name was Patty—tells me, 'Ms. Rose, I'm shy by nature. And I'm not as good looking as some of the other girls in my school. When I started my freshman year in high school, I really just wanted to blend in. I've never really gotten into trouble in the past, but when girls in my gym class invited me to party with them, I accepted their invitation. I was thrilled to finally be noticed.' She paused for a few seconds, and I could tell she was wondering if she should continue."

"So what happened?" Brad said.

"That party led to another party and to another. Her grades started to slip and her family relationships were damaged—all because she was tired of fighting alone, tired of not fitting in. Eventually, one of her friends accidentally overdosed on ecstasy at a party, and she died."

Brad winced. "How awful."

"Patty told me that 'Stand Up' came out a few days later and it not only made her question the way she was living, but it gave her the strength to make some changes."

"That's powerful," Brad said.

Sarah nodded. "I hugged her and complimented her for her strength. And then I did something that night that I had never done before, or since. I gave her my home phone number and I took hers as well. When I called to check on her a few days later, she couldn't believe it. Over twenty years later, we are still in touch and she's doing well."

"What a great story."

"I don't take any credit. My music was just one of the triggers that helped her realize an important truth. The thing is, that song hasn't been in circulation now for many years. Since it isn't modern, young girls aren't listening to my stuff anymore. I don't have all the answers, but I feel like I have more to say now than ever. I've just not been willing to try because of the way I'll feel when I sing these old songs—so many of which are about Rick."

"So that's why Alma's words hit home." He nodded, seeming to change his mind about Alma's message.

She pursed her lips and nodded.

"Maybe Alma's gift is telling the truth in love and if she had kept it to herself, then you wouldn't be considering what I think you're considering."

"Oh, you know what I'm thinking now, do you?" She smiled.

He squirmed. "I don't have an answer for that."

She burst out laughing, glad to have the upper hand again—at least for the moment.

* * *

Ray and Alma came back with the air mattresses and began setting up the den. Brad and Sarah joined them.

Ray positioned the mattress that Sarah was going to use by the fireplace and reached over to turn up the radio. "Hey everybody, listen to this."

Sarah's voice filled the room.

Sarah rolled her head back and looked heavenward. "Where did they dig this one up?" It was "Have Yourself a Merry Little Christmas."

"We are in the presence of greatness," Brad kidded.

"Oh stop. I recorded this for a Christmas movie and had forgotten all about it." Early in her career, she planned to record a Christmas album at some point. But after Rick died, she never gave it a second thought.

Megan hung up the phone and rolled back into the den. "Whoa, is that you on the radio?"

Sarah nodded.

Everybody stopped what they were doing to listen to the rest of the song, making Sarah feel self-conscious at first. But hearing a young version of herself was surprisingly invigorating—not at all what she expected. In the past, she tended to flip the station when she heard one of her old songs, but her newfound perspective, courtesy of Alma, made her feel different.

Everybody applauded as the song ended.

Sarah bowed.

"Encore," Megan said.

"Oh, that's a good idea," Alma said. "Ray, do you still have that old guitar lying around here somewhere?"

"I reckon so."

"Sarah, if he can find it, will you sing us a song?" Alma patted her hands.

"That would be incredible," Megan said.

"I haven't touched a guitar in eons. Besides, I don't know how to play any Christmas music because I never recorded any, except that song you just heard, and I didn't play any instruments on that recording."

"Ray knows how to play plenty of the classics. He can play and you can sing."

Nothing like being thrown right into the fire. Oddly, though, she yearned to perform again. What better venue than being among friends, gathered around a fireplace on a snowy Christmas Eve night?

"I can't make any promises about my guitar-playing ability, but I'm game if she is." Ray nodded toward Sarah.

"Let's do it!" Sarah said.

* * *

Ray and Sarah moved toward the window in the den. In Brad's mind, the Christmas tree nearby coupled with the snow that was sticking to the window behind Ray and Sarah would provide the perfect backdrop for their mini-concert.

Ray strummed his acoustic guitar, stopping periodically to tune a string. A few minutes later, he was ready. "What do you want to sing first?"

"How about 'Silent Night'? Do you know that one?"

He nodded and began to play it.

Sarah opened her mouth, closed her eyes, and the words just flowed.

Silent night! Holy night
All is calm all is bright
Round young virgin mother and child
Holy infant so tender and mild
Sleep in heavenly peace!
Sleep in heavenly peace!

Brad had goosebumps. He ran his hands up and down his arms. Thankfully, Sarah didn't notice. Her eyes were still closed, obviously still lost in the moment.

Silent night! Holy night!
Shepherds quake at the sight

Glories stream from heaven afar
Heavenly hosts sing Hallelujah
Christ the Savior is born!
Christ the Savior is born!

Sarah opened her eyes, and Brad saw purpose in them.

Silent night! Holy night!
Son of God love's pure light
Radiant beams from thy holy face
With the dawn of redeeming grace,
Jesus, Lord at thy birth,
Jesus, Lord at thy birth.

Silent night! Holy night!
Shepherds quake at the sight
Glories stream from heaven afar
Heavenly hosts sing Hallelujah
Christ the Savior is born!
Christ the Savior is born!

Everyone applauded.

Brad could see Sarah's eyes getting moist, and who could blame her? For the first time in many years, she was doing the very thing she was put on this earth to do.

"Do you know 'The Little Drummer Boy'? I love that song," Megan said.

"I don't think I know all the words."

Within twenty seconds, Megan had found the lyrics on her iPhone. She handed it to Sarah, and Sarah nodded at Ray.

He began tapping on his guitar with his fist as a lead-in, and

112

then picked at the strings, as if he were playing a banjo. He took his time, letting the song build toward the first verse, until finally, he arrived. Sarah sang the song effortlessly, while Ray hummed softly behind her. It was a breathtaking performance from Brad's perspective.

He would never forget this Christmas. Not only was he surrounded by a small community of people who were growing closer than any team he had ever played for, but he was part of Sarah Rose's musical rebirth, and he might just be part of her real world afterward. It sounded perfect, except for Wilmington ... and Nashville.

Just enjoy the moment. You might never experience another one like it.

Chapter 16

The impromptu concert continued long into the night. The snow continued to fall behind Ray and Sarah as they played in the shadows of the flickering candlelight.

Suddenly, Megan had an idea. Between songs, she retrieved her phone from Sarah and returned to her spot. When Sarah began the next song, Megan held her phone up, turned it sideways, and hit the record button. She would ask for Sarah's permission before posting anything to YouTube, but she knew that if she got it, the clip would be all over social media and broadcast media in a matter of minutes, relaunching Sarah's career before she even left the inn.

Sarah made eye contact with Megan, appearing to take notice of Megan shooting the video, but she gave her no indication that she should stop. Megan held her phone steady as Sarah sang "White Christmas," "Silver Bells," "O Come, O Come, Emmanuel," and "Chestnuts Roasting on an Open Fire." She had a feeling Emmanuel would be the song that would set the music world on fire.

In Megan's opinion, Sarah had been reserved and self-conscious about singing in front of the group when she first started, but partway through Emmanuel, she lifted her hands and let loose. *Oh yeah, this is the song that will reintroduce Sarah Rose to the world.*

After the performance, Alma pointed them back toward the nook for sandwiches and more treats, if they so desired. Brad was the only one who took her up on her offer.

Megan pulled Sarah aside to tell her about her idea. "I feel like it was one of the most beautiful performances I've ever seen. If I upload it to YouTube, it'll jumpstart your comeback, assuming you want that."

Sarah shifted her weight. "But we didn't have any microphones and it was so dark in here."

Megan hit the play button and let the video speak for itself.

Sarah nodded. "Go ahead and post it."

Megan wrote a description of the video and hit the upload button. She texted her roommates at Creighton, asking them to spread the word about the video on social media before posting it on her own channels. Twenty minutes later, Megan checked YouTube and was stunned to see that more than 5,000 people had already viewed it. She hit refresh and the number of views jumped another 200 ... 500 ... 1,100. Megan nodded her approval.

Alma had switched the radio back on as everybody mingled for the next ten minutes, enjoying the Christmas music in the background.

"We have some exciting news to share with you," the DJ said between songs. "It involves new music from Sarah Rose. I'll have more details after this break."

"What in the world?" Brad said.

Megan filled him in on the details.

After the break, the DJ broke the news. "A video was posted on YouTube just thirty minutes ago of Sarah Rose performing here in southern Colorado. She performed 'O Come, O Come, Emmanuel' for what appears to be a small crowd in an area lodge. Someone captured the performance on video and uploaded it.

"It's the first known footage of Rose singing since the death of her husband in 1994. Let me tell you, folks, her voice is as strong as ever. Does this mean we can dare to hope for a comeback from Sarah? I'm going to post a link to the video on our website and Facebook page. You won't want to miss it. But in the meantime, I'm going to let you hear the song. The sound quality isn't the highest, but I'm sure you won't mind. Here is Ms. Sarah Rose."

He played the song and everyone in the lodge cheered.

* * *

Sarah had let her guard down, being vulnerable in front of people she had only met a day ago, and they extended nothing but mercy toward her. Maybe it was because they had their own issues they were dealing with. But Ray and Alma created the environment for it to happen, and she would be forever grateful.

Ray helped Alma put the finishing touches on the bedding. As they went about their duties, Sarah noticed a distant look on Megan's face. She directed Megan into the nook and they both took a seat in the dark.

"Thanks again for posting that video," Sarah said. "None of this technology even existed when my career was in full swing."

"I'm just happy you let me share it with the world."

"You seem a bit distracted. Is everything okay?"

"I'm just thinking about an opportunity a friend offered me." Megan picked at the padding on one of the arms of her wheelchair.

Sarah didn't want to intrude or offer unsolicited advice. After all, who was she to offer advice about anything? But she was drawn to this young woman, and she wanted to help her if she could. "Do you want to talk about it?"

Megan explained her financial situation to Sarah. "It's just been tough since my grandparents died, you know? I'm working my way through dental school so I can become a dental assistant or a dental hygienist, but I'm accumulating a ton of tuition debt as I go, and I barely make enough to survive in a house I share near campus with three other girls."

"And your friend's offer will alleviate your financial pressure?"

"My best friend, Rebecca—the one I was going to spend the holidays with—she owns a B & B in Chama and she wants me to become her assistant manager. Room and board would be free and I would be making more money than I am right now. Chama does have a college, but it might not offer the certificate I need, depending on the career path I choose. But Farmington is what, maybe a hundred miles away? I could get my certificate through a college there, taking most of my classes online."

"That sounds perfect."

"Except that I would be required to make that drive once a week to meet some in-class requirements. It's doable, for sure, but if I ever needed to stay over in Farmington for some reason, I couldn't afford it."

Sarah placed a hand on Megan's right knee. "That's an easy fix. You can stay with me. I'd love to see you on a weekly basis. And when I need to go back to Nashville, which is a real possibility, to record or for various events, you can stay in my place while I'm gone. I'll give you a key and you can come and go as you please."

"That's incredible. Thank you!"

It was Megan's turn to cry.

Chapter 17

The next morning, Alma heard faint stirring in the den, so she approached the sleeping masses. "Lukewarm coffee, anyone?"

Sarah stretched her arms and legs on her air mattress and forced her eyes open. "Coffee?"

"Forgot I had some instant in the cupboard. I bought it for occasions just like this. Unfortunately, I had no way to heat it, so I ran the tap water as hot as it would go. Hopefully, it'll serve its purpose, but you better get it quick."

That was enough incentive to get everybody up and moving.

The hair on the side of Brad's head stuck straight out. It was the first time Alma had seen him without his ball cap. She was surprised he didn't sleep in it.

Apparently, coffee was more important to the guests than morning breath because they all opted for it before freshening up. Alma always loved to see guests first thing in the morning because it showed a different side of them. Some woke up slowly, like Brad. Others were ready to take on the day first thing, like Megan—who was already fidgeting with her phone. Since she wasn't able to charge it overnight, she would probably be going through technology withdrawals soon.

"Whoa!" Megan stared at her screen. "The video went viral.

It has more than a million views." She looked at Sarah, who was just getting up. "I bet the media is going crazy trying to reach you."

Sarah stood and stretched her arms heavenward. "They are probably calling my former manager in Nashville, but he has no way to get in touch with me now."

"You can pick and choose who you want to talk to. In fact, you could handpick one print or broadcast journalist—or maybe even a blogger—and make his or her career by scoring an exclusive with you. Or, you could take the shotgun approach and book a bunch of interviews in a row."

"I need coffee," Sarah said. "And how do you know such things?"

"I'm twenty. Everybody my age knows these things. So, what do you think? Was there a journalist who covered you in the past who stands out in your mind—somebody you might want to offer an exclusive?"

Sarah closed her eyes and took a sip of coffee. "None that I can think of, but you're right, I either need to make a statement or grant an interview."

"Do you know what you're going to say, dear?" Alma said.

"I'll just tell the truth and then be as vague as possible about my future since I have no idea what it will look like."

Alma passed around a plate of glazed donuts.

"My jeans already fit a little tighter and I've only been here a couple of days." Sarah slipped her thumb inside her waistband and tugged. But she took a donut anyway.

"That's alright, dear. You'll work it off onstage."

Alma was pleased to see the progress Sarah had made already, but she wondered about Brad and Megan. Neither had a breakthrough yet, but they still had the entire day for that to happen. And Christmas Day was the perfect day for it.

Brad had been more willing to let his guard down than she expected. But she suspected that he was overthinking things with Sarah. She could see it in the tension on his face and in his restlessness last night. Long after the other two guests fell asleep, he tossed and turned, clearly bothered by something. Given everything he said about not being there for Karen and his children, he was probably wondering how he could possibly manage a baseball team so far away while also being with Sarah, but this wasn't an either/or situation. Hopefully, he would come to that understanding before he left.

Megan seemed different last night after her conversation with Sarah. So far, Megan hadn't let on that she was struggling with a decision, but that's the only reason she was at Mercy Inn. She was wounded and in need of healing before she could move on to the next phase of her life.

Ray pulled the door to the lodge open and stomped his boots in the entryway, trying to get all the snow off them. "It has stopped snowing, but the wind is brutal. The path to your cabin is clear, Megan. I also cleared a path to both of your cabins." He pointed toward Brad and Sarah. "But don't stray off those paths. At least one of the electrical lines is down. There could be more. Grab anything you want or need from your cabin, and come on back to the lodge where I'll have a new fire roaring in no time."

They left the lodge in a group, with Brad pushing Megan. Alma couldn't help but smile after the door closed. "Don't you love to see the changes in people every year? It never gets old."

"At least nobody is rebelling this year." Ray removed the rest of his winter wear and hung it up on the coat rack. "All we can do is point them toward the truth. They have to take it from there."

Alma nodded. "I'm just enjoying the way these three are bonding, even if two of them haven't had breakthroughs yet." She cleared the breakfast dishes and wiped the counters and tabletops. When the guests returned, she pointed them toward the private bathroom in the lodge so they could shower. Today would be a big day. She hoped.

* * *

Megan got ready first. As soon as she finished, she grabbed her phone and began searching for the perfect person to interview Sarah. Not really being a big country music fan, she didn't know where to start, but after a few minutes of Googling various phrases, she found plenty of media outlets to comb through. And she had this nagging feeling that she was supposed to find a writer who needed a break. An exclusive interview with Sarah Rose would certainly do the trick, especially in light of the way her video was being received.

Megan found several websites and blogs that were clearly in it for the traffic—filled with gossip and sexy top ten lists designed to capitalize on people's never-ending desire for such things. She ruled them out and kept searching.

Megan's friends in high school—the few she had—always made fun of her for not caring about the latest Hollywood gossip. She had a hard time understanding why anybody would care about which star was dating another star, or what a star had for lunch. She would rather know what inspired them.

The battery icon on her iPhone turned red. After several more failed attempts to find the right site, she found one called *The Belt Buckle*—a blog that was written by a passionate country music fan named Jake Thrower. He lived in Nashville and wrote long articles about why certain songs meant something to him. He also had a few interviews on the site with up-and-coming country singers. He had a nice, simple design, and advertisers were beginning to notice his work. *Imagine what an interview with Sarah could do for him?*

Megan sent him an email offering him an interview with one of the biggest country music stars of the past twenty-five years, without revealing Sarah's name. She included her phone number, saying time was of the essence. After she hit send, she hoped she hadn't jumped the gun. She should have checked with Sarah first, but since she had been out of the industry for so long, she didn't have a media outlet preference.

Megan's phone rang just as Sarah walked back into the lodge from the private living quarters after getting ready.

"Jake, thanks for calling so quickly."

"When someone makes an offer like the one you just made, how could I not jump at that opportunity? Who you got?"

"I can't tell you just yet, but I'll have her call you shortly. Maybe five minutes, okay?"

After Megan ended the call, she motioned to Sarah. "Don't be mad."

"Famous first words."

At least she is smiling. "I found the perfect person to interview you." Megan filled her in on the details about Jake and his blog, pointing out that he's all about the music, not celebrity gossip.

"A girl after my own heart. I can't tell you how many paparazzi and scummy journalists I dealt with back in the day. Thanks for finding someone who breaks the mold. Did you set up a time for the interview?" Sarah glanced at her watch.

"He's ready anytime. Is your phone charged up enough to make the call?"

Sarah glanced at her phone. "My battery is at thirty-eight percent. I'm good."

Megan jotted down Jake's number on a napkin and handed it to Sarah.

Sarah asked Alma if she could go somewhere quiet for twenty minutes for the phone interview and Alma took her to an office back in the private living quarters.

* * *

Sarah ended the call, feeling satisfied. Megan had chosen the right person for the job. Jake asked deep, heartfelt questions and she was happy to answer them. Halfway through the call, Brad had walked by. And then the lights came back on in the lodge, so Ray must have restarted the generator. A light came on inside her mind as well.

When Sarah returned to the nook in the lodge, Megan was plugging in her phone charger. Brad and Ray chatted near the door, pointing at something outside.

"Thank you for setting that up," Sarah said to Megan. "It went really well."

"Glad to help."

"You're really good at this."

Megan set her phone on one of the nearby tables to let it charge. "It was fun."

"Look, I know you're mulling over an offer from Rebecca and

that may be a great fit for you. But you know social media really well. And you obviously used your skills to find the perfect interviewer for me to talk to a few minutes ago. I know we haven't known each other long, but I've seen enough to trust you."

"I haven't heard that very often in my life." Megan pursed her lips.

"I want you to be my personal manager."

Megan's mouth opened, but nothing came out.

"You would be my gatekeeper. No media, no fan request, and no charity event gets to me without going through you first. You would travel with me when I'm touring, and live in Farmington the rest of the time—either with me or somewhere on your own, whichever you prefer. And I would want you to continue to pursue whichever dental certificate you choose. I don't know how we'll make all of that work, but we'll figure it out. Oh, and I would provide you with a six-figure salary, and I'll cover your tuition."

Megan began to weep.

Sarah put her arms around her and held her close.

Brad and Ray stopped talking to see what the commotion was all about. Sarah raised her hand toward them as if to say everything was okay.

Sarah held Megan until she got her emotions under control. Even at the age of twenty, Megan really was the perfect fit for the job. Sarah knew she could hire more experienced managers, or maybe even her previous one, but she just had a feeling about Megan—it was as if she knew from the time she met her that she was supposed to do something for her. In this scenario, they would be helping one another.

But she also knew Megan had another option on the table. At

least Sarah had done her part by offering her the opportunity of a lifetime—one that would allow Megan the ability to provide for herself.

Chapter 18

They resumed their game of Nicebreaker shortly after ten o'clock in the morning. Ray chose Alma and asked her: "Dogs or cats? Why?" Megan didn't hear her answer. She rehashed her conversation with Sarah over and over in her mind. This was the break some people waited for their entire lives and she was getting hers at such a young age. She felt guilty at first, but that quickly turned to gratitude.

After Alma finished speaking, Brad asked if they could turn on the TV to get an update on the weather forecast. When Ray turned the TV on, one of the local channels was showing a day-time talk show with a running scroll at the bottom: "Repeating ... all major thoroughfares in the following counties remain closed: Rio Grande, Alamosa, Huerfano, Conejos, Costilla, and Las Animas ... including I-25 south of Walsenburg all the way to the New Mexico border. Some areas in these counties have received more than twenty-four inches of snow. Crews are working around the clock to clear the roads. I-25 will reopen tomorrow morning at 8:00 o'clock. Stay tuned for further announcements."

Ray turned off the TV. "We are in Conejos County. From the sounds of things, Highway 17 may not be open tomorrow morning. But that doesn't mean it won't open later in the day.

127

They always focus on I-25 first though."

For the first time since arriving, Megan didn't have any sense of urgency to leave. Besides, what would she tell Rebecca if the roads did reopen tomorrow? Or Sarah, for that matter?

* * *

Megan asked the group to skip her and they obliged, making it Sarah's turn. She picked Brad and flipped the card over. "Who is the first person who comes to mind when you hear a love song on the radio?"

Brad sighed. "Can I answer Alma's question instead?"

"I don't think that's how it works, and you aren't getting off the hook that easily." Sarah smirked.

"Well, my answer isn't as easy as this question makes it sound." He tugged on his baseball cap. "If the song is about young love, then I think about Karen. If the song is about being with someone forever, I don't think of anybody, which totally bums me out, so I usually change the channel."

"What about an angry love song like 'Wasting All These Tears' by Cassadee Pope?" Sarah raised her eyebrows, showing too much interest.

"I can't relate to tha—"

A crack appeared in the ceiling over the couch. Everybody looked up just as the ceiling gave way. From that point on, everything was a blur. The roof collapsed on Sarah and Megan, burying them in snow and debris. Alma screamed. Ray shot out of his chair, followed closely by Brad.

Brad dug for Megan while Ray focused on Sarah.

Megan moaned but he couldn't hear anything from Sarah. Instinctively, the two men began digging through the debris. Brad cut his hand on a nail and blood ran down his arm, but he didn't stop digging. The temperature in the room dropped sixty degrees or more, Brad guessed, in just a matter of seconds. Not only did the temperature drop, but the wind dipped inside, making their situation even more volatile.

"Megan?" Brad could see her arm. "Are you conscious?"

"I think my ... leg is broken."

"Okay, hang on. We're coming for you."

Alma dropped to her knees and began to pray. Sarah and Megan would need every prayer she said if they were going to survive.

Brad needed to find a way to remove the debris without hurting Megan further. He hoped Ray was making progress with freeing Sarah. If the men didn't get to them quickly, both women could freeze to death.

A surge of anger rushed through Brad's body. How could this happen right after Sarah finally decided to begin recording again? And clearly, something special had happened between Sarah and Megan just a few minutes prior, which made Megan happier than he had seen her since they met. Brad believed in God, but sometimes he questioned His timing. But was there ever really a good time to have a roof collapse on a person? He shivered as the wind cut into his skin.

Alma raced over to the coat rack and brought the men their coats. "Put them on. Now!"

Both men ignored her, at first.

"Now!"

They relented and shoved their arms inside as quickly as they could. Then, without saying another word, the men worked frantically to free the women.

The cut on Brad's hand began to throb. He glanced down at it and noticed a gash more than an inch long on his palm. He pushed beyond the pain, knowing two human lives were at stake. He couldn't let them down.

Ray's stamina surprised Brad. *He must be running on adrenaline. I know I am.* Ray grabbed a couple of two-by-fours and hurled them aside.

Brad removed a large section of plaster and one of the nails opened another gash on the same hand. They were getting close. They had to be.

"I hear something." Ray pointed under the debris. "It's a moan."

That only fueled their adrenaline.

Alma, who was back on her knees, began to pray aloud. "Father, thank you for protecting Sarah and Megan. Help us to rescue them so we might nurse them back to health. Give us speed, precision, and the energy to overcome."

Brad removed another piece of plaster and reached Megan. Once her other arm was free, she reached for her leg. She was right. It was broken.

* * *

Megan closed her eyes. Pain shot down her leg and up through her hip. And she was cold. So cold.

"Hang in there, girl," Brad said. "We'll have you out in no time. Does anything else hurt?"

"I don't think so."

"I need to be extremely careful when I pull you free. We don't want to cause any more injuries."

She nodded and tried to sit up, but the blinding pain sent her straight to her back again.

Ray came over to help, putting one of his hands out. "Don't move, Megan. We'll get you out of here." His smile was convincing.

"What about Sarah?"

"We'll come back and get her as soon as you're safe and sound," Ray said.

Megan shivered from the drop in temperature.

"You ready to get out of here?" Brad said.

She nodded.

He reached down and wrapped his arms around her back and just below her bottom, careful not to touch her broken leg. Ray grabbed a nearby pillow and came around the other side to support her leg until they could get her to safety.

When Brad began to lift Megan, she screamed.

* * *

Sarah heard a scream and opened her eyes. *Where am I? What happened?* She knew she was trapped under debris—was it in the lodge? *The crack in the ceiling ... the roof must have caved in from all the snow.* She turned her head to the left, then the right, but all she could see was darkness. She didn't feel any pain, but she wasn't going anywhere until help arrived. *Is everyone buried in this? Oh God, please don't let anybody die.*

"Help!" she said. "Can anybody hear me?"

She paused for a response.

"We're coming for you, Sarah," Alma said.

Alma's tone was more excitable than Sarah had ever heard her.

"Am I the only one who is trapped? Who just screamed?"

"We've already uncovered Megan and got her to safety, dear." It sounded like Alma was removing debris from above and tossing it aside. "The two men will be back in a minute and we'll get you out. Are you injured?"

Sarah could move her legs. They appeared to be free. But her left arm was pinned to the ground. Her pinky and ring fingers on that hand throbbed.

"I think I have a couple of broken fingers, but nothing serious that I can tell." Her right arm was free. She tried to free her left arm, but she couldn't budge the debris.

Every few seconds, moisture dripped down through the tangled mess and landed on her face. She fought the urge to panic.

Alma continued to work on the debris and just as the men were returning, Alma lifted a section of plaster and she made eye contact with Sarah. "There you are, dear. You're going to be just fine."

The two men rushed to Sarah's side and gently removed the section of the ceiling that had pinned Sarah's arm.

She flexed her arm once it was free and examined her broken fingers. Her injuries were minor compared to what might have been.

"Are you able to stand?" Brad asked. "Are you hurt?"

Sarah braced herself with her right hand and pushed herself up, expecting to feel pain somewhere, but she didn't.

She inspected her body. "I have lots of scrapes, cuts, and

bruises, but I don't think I have any major injuries. I'm still a little sore from the car accident, so it's hard to know which injury is related to which accident." She shivered.

"Here you go, dear." Alma smothered her with a blanket. "We need to get you out of the cold." She led Sarah to the private living quarters.

* * *

Megan repositioned herself on the couch in the private living quarters in an apparent attempt to get comfortable, wincing with every movement. Sarah was settled into a rocking chair, having already been tended to by Alma, who taped her two broken fingers together. Brad had plopped down in Ray's weathered recliner.

"I'm going to call 911 to see if they can send a life-flight helicopter out here," Ray said to Megan.

She nodded.

He picked up his cell phone and placed the call to report Megan's condition.

"I'm afraid that the life-flight helo has been grounded until the high winds cease," the 911 operator said. "How serious is her injury?"

"Well, I'm not a doctor, but her leg is broken. I think that's the extent of it, but I cannot be certain."

"We should be able to get one into the air shortly after the wind ceases, but we only have one helo. We'll have to prioritize patients when we're cleared to fly again."

"Fair enough, I'll call back when the wind dies down and we'll go from there." Ray ended the call.

"I got the gist of it," Megan said. "Thanks."

"Sure thing. In the meantime, we need to keep your leg as stable as possible, so get comfy, because we are going to baby you."

* * *

Megan's leg, which was fractured just below the knee, was beginning to swell and turn brown, yellow, and green. She was in for a long night, but her new friends would keep her company. She wouldn't forget this Christmas any time soon. It changed her life, in more ways than one.

"We have about four hours of electricity left in the generator," Ray announced. "If everybody's set, I'm going to head back over to the guest side of the inn to turn off everything that uses electricity so we can make our propane supply last as long as possible." When nobody spoke, he disappeared. Brad followed him, saying he was going to see if Megan's wheelchair survived.

"While we have electricity, I'm going to take advantage of it and make a Christmas dinner to remember," Alma said.

Sarah offered to help, but Alma waved her off.

"Sit. Rest. I'll have a meal whipped up in no time." Alma headed for the kitchen.

* * *

Megan's wheelchair was a tangled mess—beyond repair, so Brad left it in the debris and returned to the private living quarters where he gave Megan the news. She seemed unfazed by it, which made sense given how much worse the situation could have been.

Brad flipped the transistor radio on for a weather update and learned that not much had changed. Many in the area were without power. That was good news and bad news, from Brad's perspective. Bad because so many would be struggling without a generator and therefore in dire need of immediate help. Good because authorities would surely call in help from around the area to clear the roads to get the power restored and to rescue those who needed it.

An hour later, Alma set out a modest plate of cold cuts for lunch, renewing her promise for a tasty Christmas dinner later. Sarah fixed Megan's plate and brought it to her. They ate in silence, mostly—still in shock over what had happened.

Sarah finished her sandwich and dropped her paper plate into the trash can. "Can I take a look at your leg?"

"Be my guest, but it's not pretty."

Sarah raised the bag of ice and blanket. "Are you in a lot of pain?"

"The pain medicine Alma gave me is helping. I've gone through multiple surgeries and recoveries in my life, so I'm used to pain."

Sarah put the blanket down, setting the bag of ice back on top. "Let me know if I can get you anything, sweetie."

"You're starting to sound like Alma."

"She's good people, so maybe she's starting to rub off on me."

This was the closest thing to extended family Brad had ever

135

felt. His Aunt Julie did the best she could in raising Denise and him, but the three of them never really bonded as a family. Aunt Julie already had an established life. Denise went her way in high school and he went his.

Even after he got married and had children, he was gone too often to ever fully bond with his family. But in two short days, he learned what he had been missing—trust, honesty, pain, laughter. The weight of this realization wore heavily on him. He needed to call Ryan and Amy. He hoped Amy would pick up this time—especially on Christmas Day.

Chapter 19

egan's phone buzzed on the nightstand next to the couch. She picked it up and saw that she had received an email from Jake. He already posted the interview and provided a link. Megan clicked on it and read the story.

Exclusive Interview: Sarah Rose Ready to Make a Comeback

If you're a country music fan, then you've seen the video of Sarah Rose performing "O Come, O Come, Emmanuel" in a remote cabin in southern Colorado that appeared on YouTube yesterday and has already garnered some 3.5 million views. It created a firestorm of speculation about Rose's possible return to the country music world. She stepped away twenty-two years ago, after the death of her husband.

[Jake inserted a copy of the video into the story.]

Since this video went viral, I was contacted by a woman who is close to Rose and offered The Belt Buckle *the opportunity to interview her to set the record straight about why she stepped away from the music industry, and why she was ready to make a comeback. I spoke to Ms. Rose earlier today and here's what she had to say.*

First, thank you for choosing The Belt Buckle as your way of communicating with country music fans.

Thank you for having me, Jake.

So tell us about the video. What's the story behind it?

I was on my way to visit my mom in Colorado Springs for the holidays when I ran into a blizzard in southern Colorado. I slid off the road right in front of a quaint little inn and hunkered down inside. The roads are closed in the area, so I've gotten to know the other residents really well. We decided to make the best of things and enjoy the holidays together.

As we were listening to Christmas music in the background and playing a game, one of my old Christmas songs came on the radio. One of the residents asked me to sing for the group and I did. The video you see was just an impromptu decision by one of the guests to record it. Of course, she got my permission to post it.

It sounds like you're experiencing quite an ordeal there so you've probably been too busy to keep up with the buzz your video performance created, but fans are asking whether this is just a one-time event, or if it

will launch your comeback.

Well, since we didn't plan to shoot the video, there was no forethought about the purpose of it—at least on my part. My associate, Megan, was privy to some information, though, and began to shoot the video with that in mind.

We're dying to know what that information is ...

In recent months, I've had the creative itch for the first time since Rick died. That, coupled with a conversation I had with a friend here at the inn, helped me realize my music doesn't belong to me. It belongs to the people it helps through the rough patches of life. I decided right then that I was going to make a comeback. I don't have any details yet, but I plan to begin writing new material right away.

That's great news. Can we expect to see a subsequent tour?

I'd be lying if I said I wasn't nervous about touring. I know that fans will want to hear their old favorites, and I have every intention of singing them, but this is going to be a process for me. Understand that I wrote many of those songs about Rick. So going onstage every night and singing them will be opening up some old wounds. But I can honestly say that I'm experiencing healing right now and I think that will allow me to press on.

Do you want to talk about the healing process? What

has that looked like?

I'm not sure I fully understand it, yet. My answer to Rick's death was to run. I've been living on a ranch in New Mexico for the past twenty-two years with no intention of resurfacing. I could have lived out my days there without ever stepping back into the limelight. In a sense, I hit the pause button on my life and on the healing process. In my mind, that was better than the alternative, which involved a lot of pain.

You have to understand that I was really just a kid when Rick died. I was twenty-two years old, newly married, and a bit naive. That's not to say I didn't struggle early on to find a record deal, but after I got one, my first album did really well and that led to opportunities to open for some artists with big names. By the time that tour ended, my record company was clamoring for a second album.

After the second album went multi-platinum, I was headlining my own tour and selling out arenas. After avoiding the sophomore slump, my third album sold even more copies and the sold-out arenas continued. I knew enough to realize all of this could change overnight. You can never take success for granted. And, I have to admit, I always feared losing the muse. That's exactly what happened when Rick died.

For the first time in my professional life, I was dealing with loss and pain, and I didn't know how to cope with it, so I decided to run and I've been running ever since.

But the people I've met at this inn have reawakened my desire for music.

You should meet Megan—she has cerebral palsy and has very little support, but she's still going to college to pursue a career and finding a way to scrape by. Her strength encourages me, and in a way, it's helping me to face my own challenges.

And then there's this guy here named Brad. He was a minor league baseball player his entire career. He never made it to the big leagues. But now he's about to become a minor league manager, which will begin a new fight to make it to the big leagues. I'm inspired by his tenacity, and, like with Megan, seeing his strength just speaks to me.

Finally, the lovely elderly couple who run this inn have been a godsend to me. Without their support, I wouldn't have ever decided to make a comeback.

So, in a way, things have come full circle for you. Your music touched people and helped them through difficult times all those years ago, and now this elderly couple is doing the same for you.

I hadn't looked at it that way, but you make a good point. That sort of makes us dependent on one another then, doesn't it?

I believe it does. Is there anything else you would like

to add or address?

*Patience would be appreciated. I haven't written any-
thing or recorded in years. I'm making a comeback, but
I'm not the naive twenty-two-year-old I was the last
time you saw me. I'm broken, battered, and just trying
to hang on like everybody else.*

Megan reread the interview several times. She was moved by
Sarah's authenticity and willingness to be so open about where
she was right now. And knowing that Sarah drew strength from
her brought a tear to her eye.

She scrolled to the bottom of the blog post, noting that it
already had more than a thousand comments, mostly from
well-wishers. But like with anything else online, there were a
few detractors who hid behind anonymity. That was the price
of being a public figure these days. She was going to have to try
to shield Sarah from this side of technology.

* * *

Sarah checked on Megan's leg periodically, while Alma prepared dinner in the kitchen. Megan's leg continued to swell,
but she said the pain medicine was doing the trick for now.
Getting her to the bathroom was out of the question, so they
would have to figure out a way to facilitate her needs while also
respecting her privacy.

Ray flipped the transistor radio back on and set it on the coffee
table in front of Megan. "Rudolph the Red-Nosed Reindeer"

played softly in the background and Megan began to sing it. Soon, everybody else joined her.

* * *

Ray glanced out the window at the large evergreen tree he decorated with a string of colored lights a few days prior. Not a branch was moving. The storm was finally over. All that was left was the cleanup. And a quick call to 911 to check on the availability of the helicopter.

He was sad to learn from the 911 operator that quite a few people had been stranded along various highways in the area and many of them were facing hypothermia, so they were a higher priority than Megan's injury. He certainly understood that. The operator took his cell phone number and said she would call him if the helicopter became available. But she said it would probably be quicker to get an ambulance out to the inn the next morning once the roads were cleared.

"Thank you," Ray said. "We'll just plan on calling for an ambulance then."

He filled Megan in on the details.

Over the next few hours, Ray and Brad surveyed the damage in the den, cleared the pathways to the cabins one final time, and they checked the generator. It had to be running on fumes at that point—especially since Alma was cooking a big dinner and using a lot of electricity.

The road reports sounded positive. Crews were making good progress on I-25 and would be hitting the highways soon. The guests would indeed be leaving the next day.

* * *

Once Ray and Brad settled back into the living room, they resumed their game of Nicebreaker, determining that it was Megan's turn.

She chose Ray. "Do you believe in angels? If so, have you ever encountered one?"

This wasn't the first time he had received this question over the years. It was one of the originals and it always sparked an interesting conversation. He took a seat in a recliner and put his feet up. "Of course I believe in angels. They are mentioned more than 200 times in the Bible and they serve all sorts of different functions; they are messengers, ministers, protectors, guardians, and warriors."

"Have you ever seen one?" Megan asked.

"The book of Hebrews says we are not to neglect to show hospitality to strangers, for thereby some have entertained angels unawares. So you never know when you're ministering to an angel."

"That doesn't really answer Megan's question," Sarah said.

"We rarely know when we've seen an angel, but yes, I have seen angels—many times."

"Care to elaborate?" Brad said. He had taken up residence in the rocking chair Alma usually sat in.

How could he word this in a way they would understand? He'd always been able to avoid the second part of the question in the past. He wasn't authorized to reveal everything to them, and he couldn't lie to them. "Anybody who has been on this earth as long as I have has seen an angel or two in his day, if he was paying attention."

The smell of turkey swirled through the room.

"Oh, that smells so good," Megan said.

Saved by the turkey. Good going, Alma.

Alma appeared a few seconds later, announcing that dinner was almost ready. "I hope you saved room for a feast."

Chapter 20

Sarah couldn't believe her eyes when she walked into the kitchen. Somehow, Alma had found a way to whip up a turkey, stuffing, mashed potatoes, a green bean casserole, a huge basket of honey-glazed dinner rolls, and a pumpkin pie. "How did you pull this off in such a short time?"

"I've been doing this a long time, dear. I know my way around a kitchen. And, truth be told, the turkey was precooked and the pie was frozen—but you better not tell a soul." Alma winked at Sarah and opened a cupboard, removing what appeared to be her best china. She set it on the table. "Would you mind stirring the mashed potatoes, dear?"

"Sure thing."

"The turkey will be done soon. I know it's early, but Ray says the generator will be shutting off any minute, so I wanted to get dinner ready as soon as possible."

"How much longer will the turkey take?"

"Thirty minutes. But it's close enough that if the generator does go off that I could leave the bird in the oven and the heat would finish the job."

Sarah nodded.

"So, why don't we go back into the living room with the others," Alma said. "We're done in here for now. We can set out a few TV trays since we'll be serving the meal family style."

* * *

"Whose turn is it for Nicebreaker?" Megan would never admit it, but she loved the conversation that the game generated.

"Brad? I think you're up," Ray said.

Brad chose Megan. "If you had to move to a different state, where would you move and why?"

Megan ran her hand along her leg under the blanket. "I'm actually going to be moving to New Mexico soon. The question is, which job will I take?" She raised her eyebrows in Sarah's direction as a way to ask Sarah's permission to tell everyone about her offer.

Sarah nodded.

Megan explained her options—she could move in with Rebecca and help her run her B & B in Farmington or she could move in with Sarah and become her assistant.

"Based on the way you handled Sarah's video, and then setting up the interview for her, becoming her assistant makes perfect sense." Brad drummed his fingers on the arms of his rocking chair. "But it sounds like you have two very good options to choose from."

"Helping Rebecca would be fun. And I'd love to be around her every day. We were close and I've missed her so much since she moved. But becoming Sarah's assistant just feels right, you know? I feel like I was born to do that type of work. I've been floundering for years, not knowing what I wanted to do with my life. I figured becoming a dental hygienist would be a good choice, so I set the wheels in motion. But it took this trip—this encounter with all of you, to help me see what I really want to do."

Sarah patted her hands. "Does that mean you're accepting my offer?"

"I am."

* * *

When Mercy Inn lost power, Brad was actually grateful for the cover of darkness, given what he was about to do. He needed to talk to Sarah. Now. He didn't know how she would respond to an invitation to the kitchen in the private living quarters, but he invited her anyway. She seemed happy to accept.

They took a seat at the kitchen table—hardly the most romantic spot in the world, but sometimes you have to improvise. He offered Sarah a cup of Christmas Delight and poured her a cup, and then one for himself. The time for stalling was over.

"I know we haven't known each other long, but I can't let you walk out of here tomorrow without telling you I think you're a special woman." He stared at the table before getting up the nerve to look her in the eye.

She was fixated on his hand though. "Before we get into all of that, your hand is bleeding right through the bandage." She reached over and drew his hand toward her to peel the bandage back so she could take a better look. "Let me rinse it off for you." She got up and rummaged through the cupboards. "Where did Alma store the first aid kit after she taped my fingers together?"

She finally found it, but Brad couldn't help but wonder if she was stalling too—looking for the right words.

She removed his bandage and ran his hand under cold water, using only her good hand.

Her touch was electric.

"I was apprehensive about you at first—thinking you might be another overzealous fan." Sarah patted his hand dry with a clean towel. "But you've been so honest about your past mistakes that you put me at ease. You're a good man, Brad, even though you don't seem to believe that." She patted his hand dry and applied two band-aids, covering them with a new gauze bandage.

They both took a seat at the table, facing each other. He could hardly breathe, much less speak. It reminded him of how he felt when he asked Karen out for the first time all those years ago.

"The way you interacted with Megan was beautiful to watch." Sarah tucked a strand of hair behind her ear. "I don't know what the two of you were talking about, but your tenderness toward her really touched me. And the way you talk about your kids. I love that. Even the way you show respect for Karen is impressive."

"So where does that leave us?" He ran his thumbnail along one of the grooves in the table. "I want more, just so you know. But I'm just about to start a new job some 800 miles away from Nashville."

She wrinkled her nose. "What does Nashville have to do with anything?"

"Won't you be moving back there?"

"I'll have to visit on occasion, but I have no plans to move from my ranch."

"Ah, okay. Well, Wilmington is probably more than 2,000

miles away from Farmington. That makes it even worse."

"I feel pretty confident that we can make the long-distance thing work—at least for now. We can figure out the details later."

Brad finally looked up and made eye contact with Sarah. Her eyes softened and his stomach flipped. He reached for her hand and leaned in close to kiss her. Just as their lips touched, his phone rang and they pulled apart.

"It's Amy," Brad said.

"Take it. Like I said, we can sort out the details later." She kissed him and left him alone to talk to his daughter.

* * *

"Merry Christmas, Dad," Amy said.

"And Merry Christmas to you too, honey. Sorry I couldn't make it in time."

"Ryan filled me in. Everything okay there?"

"Better than okay." He explained his accommodations but he didn't tell her about his chance meeting with Sarah. No matter how long he had been divorced from Karen, he didn't want to drag his grown children into his love life, until or unless he was in an established relationship. He promised to head to Denver as soon as the roads were clear for a belated Christmas celebration.

"That works. Ryan and I are having a blast together. He invited me to a friend's house for Christmas dinner. That's where I am right now."

"Enjoy, honey. I'll see you soon."

* * *

"Dinner time!" Alma began setting the food on the table.

Sarah helped her with the food while Ray lit a few more candles and placed them around the living room. When he was done, he began carving the turkey, humming to the tune of "Jingle Bells."

"The turkey smells awesome!" Megan said. "I can smell it all the way in here."

"It sure does, but I have my nose aimed at that pumpkin pie." Brad stood up. "Smells heavenly."

"Patience, patience." Sarah stood and patted him on the arm.

"Ray, honey, you want to say the blessing?" Alma stepped out of the kitchen and joined them.

Ray nodded and everyone bowed. "Heavenly Father, we thank you for the new friends you have brought our way this year. Thank you for allowing them to arrive safely and thank you for the new mission you have given each of them. We trust that this time away from the busyness of the world has helped to reorient them. As all of us return to our normal routines tomorrow, we ask that we would go in your strength with clear direction. Thank you for providing for us through this storm and for sparing our lives when the roof collapsed. We ask that you nourish our bodies with this food. In Jesus' name, amen."

"Amen," they said.

Alma prepared a plate for Megan and invited the others to the table.

As Sarah piled her plate full, she realized what she had been missing all these years since Rick died—the intimacy of communal meals; passing plates, chitchat, and anticipating one another's needs. All of it created a familial environment that looked considerably different than opening a boxed entrée, sticking it in the microwave, and then eating it by herself in front of the TV.

She made circles with her shoulders, trying to stretch out the soreness in her body. And then she reached for Brad's injured hand to make sure it wasn't bleeding through the new bandage. It wasn't.

After everybody's plates were full, they took a seat and dug in.

"Mmm," Sarah said. This turkey is so tender, Alma. And the rest of the food looks so good—reminds me of the meals momma used to make."

"Thank you, dear. I've just had a lot of practice, that's all. But I'm glad it's edible."

A wordless jazz version of "The Christmas Song" played in the background. Sarah hummed along.

Megan smirked. "Someone is sure in a good mood—especially for a woman who was buried in rubble not all that long ago."

Sarah glared at her but was unable to contain a smile a second later.

Chapter 21

After finishing off the pumpkin pie, Brad needed a nap, but Alma broke out the index cards again instead.

Ray indicated that it was Alma's turn. She chose Brad. "Romantically speaking, is there a difference between loving someone and being in love with someone? If so, what?"

He let out a mock sigh. "These questions are killing me."

Sarah laughed. "Don't be a wuss."

"I haven't exactly won any awards for being husband of the year, so take my answer with a grain of salt." He tugged on his baseball cap. "I imagine that being in love is the stuff chick flicks are made of—it's a feeling that comes and goes based on how much one person meets the romantic needs of another. But loving someone is less about a momentarily romantic feeling and more about choosing another person's needs above your own. And I suspect it's more about wanting to stick by somebody, maybe even despite his or her flaws."

"Not bad," Sarah said. "Even though it sounds like you're in favor of killing every girl's dream of meeting Mr. Darcy."

Megan rolled her eyes. "Oh, brother."

Brad felt heat in his cheeks. "Hey, why don't we check on the road conditions?"

"That was the worst transition, ever," Sarah said. "But I

would kind of like to know what's going on in the outside world too. We really need to get Megan to the hospital as soon as possible."

Ray turned the radio back on. " ... our top story. I-25 south of Walsenburg has already reopened. Crews are now focusing on clearing the following routes in southern Colorado by 8:00 o'clock tomorrow morning: Highway 160, Highway 550, Highway 285, Highway 84, and Highway 17."

The real world would be calling soon enough. At least he had one more evening with Sarah. It could be a while before he saw her again, but then again, he didn't have to report for spring training until February, so he had more than a month to do whatever he wanted.

Sarah would probably jump back into her career once she returned to Farmington, but maybe he could be part of that process. He'd love to see what her world looked like behind the scenes, but he didn't want to invite himself. *Might be a little early for that.*

* * *

Alma passed around a plate of cookies.

"Whenever I would go to my grandparents for the holidays as a kid, I always gained a few pounds." Sarah reached for the plate and took two cookies—one sugar and one chocolate chip. "I had a funny feeling when I met you that your cooking would be on par with my grandmother's. The problem with that is, I'm a bit older now and the weight doesn't come off as easily as it once did."

"Nonsense, honey." Alma waved her hand. "You're as thin as a rail already. Adding a few pounds won't hurt you in the least."

"Tell that to the PR people at my record label—when I actually get one." She had originally signed a four-album deal with Mercury Records. Her three studio releases, followed by a greatest hits album fulfilled her obligation. Mercury wanted her to sign an extension, but then Rick died. Technically, she didn't owe them another record, but they had always treated her well. She didn't even know the brass at Mercury anymore, but contacting them would be at the top of her list—or maybe Megan's list.

On second thought, she should probably make that call herself. She hadn't done this sort of thing for so long, she wasn't even sure how the process of interacting with record companies worked anymore. She had a feeling, though, that Megan would figure it out and bring her up to speed pretty quick.

What are the odds that I would find my career, the perfect manager, and a good guy all in one weekend after being stranded in an out-of-the-way inn?

Probably too high to calculate without some sort of divine intervention.

* * *

Megan rarely claimed to be excited about anything, but for the first time in her life, she was excited about her future. She did wonder about her recovery though. It could take months before she was fully healed, but she had a feeling Sarah was going to take care of everything and she would give her all the time she needed.

"I read your interview with Jake," Megan said to Sarah between Nicebreaker rounds. "Loved your vulnerability. Between the video and that interview, I feel like you've created quite a buzz in the entertainment industry. Jake emailed me asking if he could begin pointing record companies and other media toward me because he doesn't know what to do with all the requests."

"And so it begins," Brad said.

Sarah nodded. "Well, if you're officially on the job, then tell him to send everyone in your direction."

"I will develop several lists and filter them for you. We're also going to need to set up a Twitter, Instagram, Snapchat, and Facebook page. And what about your website—do you have one?"

"Websites weren't exactly a priority in 1994."

"Well, they are now. I'll find a company to design one ASAP. We'll need some new photos—so I'll find a photographer, videos of past performances, and you might even want to start a blog, even if they are so 2012. You could interact with fans there."

"It's a different world now." Sarah shook her head. "I hope I can keep up."

"You don't have to worry about that. That's why you hired me."

* * *

"I think it's my turn to ask a question." Ray crossed his legs and grabbed his index cards from the end table. "Sarah, you're on the hot seat. This one comes from a visitor we had here many, many years ago. He's since gone on to be with the Lord. When you come to the end of your life, what do you think you will be most proud of?"

She bit her lower lip and rearranged her sitting position. "I suppose I'm a work in progress in that area. I have loved well, but not well enough. And I have served others well, but not well enough."

Nobody said anything for a few seconds, giving her the time she needed to search for an answer. That's one thing she noticed about this exercise—Ray didn't mind awkward silence. He seemed to believe it led to contemplation. Maybe he didn't even see it as awkward. She repeated the question. "What will I be most proud of ... What will I be most proud of?"

Snowball jumped into her lap and purred, begging for attention. She was happy to provide it. She stroked his fur and he put his bottom in the air. He turned circles in her lap, trying to find the perfect spot to lie down. He finally plopped down and closed his eyes.

Sarah pointed at Snowball. "Before I try to answer this, there is no way I'm answering another bonus question."

Everybody laughed.

"You're off the hook," Ray said. "One bonus round is enough."

Sarah acknowledged his pardon with a head nod. "We have a small community center on the outskirts of Farmington. It offers arts and crafts classes for the elderly. It also offers judo classes and scout meetings for kiddos. And it hosts community events. I volunteer there in the mornings."

Snowball opened his eyes and looked up at her as if to say, "Stop talking and start petting, lady." Sarah picked up her intensity and stroked his fur.

"It's a great place for me to serve, for a number of reasons. It is mostly elderly and young people, so neither demographic recognizes me. As Sarah Donaldson, I clean the bathrooms, sweep the floors, and vacuum the carpets, and I serve food and drink at events. There's something about doing that type of work that grounds you. I can't really explain it."

Ray gave her the time to do so though.

"As much satisfaction as I got out of hearing from people who were changed by my music, I think serving people in a very real and tangible way means more to me. None of these people knew who I was. To them, I was just the average, middle-aged woman in a small mining town who serves in her local community center."

Ray nodded. "The Bible says to not let your left hand know what your right hand is doing, and that's a perfect example."

"But I don't know that I'll look back on those years when I'm on my deathbed and be proud of those moments as much as I will be able to say I was doing something that just felt right, you know?"

Brad reached for her hand and squeezed it. That certainly felt right.

Chapter 22

Pain shot through Megan's leg. The medicine was wearing off, so she asked Alma for another dose. After swallowing it, she asked Alma the next question on her index card. "Is there anything you would change about your life if you could?"

Alma didn't hesitate. "Not in the least, dear. I found the right guy for me and this business affords me the opportunity to be the woman God created me to be. I get to serve alongside Ray, and this venue has been the instrument of change in so many people's lives over the years. I can't imagine doing anything else."

Megan rubbed her leg and wondered why some people found their calling so easily while others struggled, like she did. Upbringing had something to do with it. Wise decision-making did too. But there was a mysterious element to this process that always bothered her.

Religious people she knew called it faith, but she just couldn't grasp it. And she also knew nonreligious people who seemed to understand the mystery. Did a person just need to live long enough to stumble into it, or was she missing something?

* * *

"I don't mean to pick on you, Alma, but you're up next for me too." Sarah flipped over the card. "Do you ever remember your dreams? If so, do you believe they mean anything?"

"I used to have a recurring dream. It was the subject of many journal entries." Alma rocked back and forth and closed her eyes. "In my dream, I see a Yorkshire Terrier named Mitsy. She is inside a large cage-like chain-link fence that is no more than five feet by five feet."

"Does she belong to somebody?" Megan said.

"Not that I can see. But she has everything she needs—food, water, even a small shelter to protect her from the elements. But never once has anybody ever visited her. That's what used to bother me most about the dream."

"Used to?" Sarah said.

"Ray and I talked about it many times and we have come to the conclusion that it means I am supposed to always remember those who don't have any close relationships in their lives. It's one of the many reasons I love this inn. People show up here tired and lonely, and if in some small way, Ray and I can meet their needs and make them feel less lonely, then I feel like I'm doing what I'm supposed to."

Sarah was going to miss Ray and Alma something terrible. She might just have to find a way to get "stranded" there again next Christmas. "I meant to ask you, Alma, is it the norm to only have three guests during Christmas? Seems like a shame to have twelve cabins for only three of us."

"We rarely have more than four guests during Christmas because, well, who really wants to spend Christmas alone?

Everybody is heading somewhere, but invariably a few end up here either because they have nowhere special to go or because they book the inn to avoid spending the holidays with family. But again, those are the people we really want to show up here, anyway."

* * *

"Ready for your third question in a row?" Brad asked Alma.

"Go ahead, dear."

"What is your favorite Christmas tradition, and why?"

She pointed toward the Christmas tree. "Every year, I put the crèche under the tree. I put Joseph and Mary in another room and the wise men in yet another room. Once a week, I move them closer and closer to the crèche to signify their travels toward Bethlehem. On Christmas morning, I place the baby Jesus in the manger and surround him with his parents and the wise men. I did that this morning before any of you woke up."

"Oh, I love that!" Sarah said.

"It takes me on a pilgrimage and it helps me to reflect on the birth of Christ."

"Beautiful," Sarah said.

Alma smiled. "Well, it's finally my turn to ask somebody a question. Ray, name something you want to learn how to do, and why?" She had heard him answer this question in the past, but she wondered if maybe he would answer differently this year.

"I used to say I want to learn how to type better, but I'm probably the best two-finger typist you've ever seen, so I've made peace with my typing skills," he said. "Handwriting just feels more natural for me. I have handwritten many journals over the years. In fact, after all of you leave, I'll be handwriting an entire account of what happened here this year."

"Oh, it would be so much fun to go back to the beginning to read all of those stories," Sarah said.

Alma couldn't help but smile. *If she only knew.*

"Every year, God seems to bring order out of chaos among the patrons here." Ray waved his hands around. "It's beautiful to behold."

"So, if typing is off the table for new skills, what do you want to learn now?" Brad scratched his chin.

Ray made eye contact with Megan. "Well, I'm hoping I type well enough to learn how to blog on the Mercy Inn website. Of course, I wouldn't get personal with guests' personal stories or anything like that, unless they gave me permission. But I'd love to find a way to put what happens here out into the world so others could read it."

"I'll have you blogging before we leave tomorrow," Megan said.

Ray's face lit up.

* * *

"If memory serves me right, that leaves us with just one question remaining," Ray said. "This one is for Megan." He smiled and flipped over his remaining card. "If you could be anywhere else but here, where would you be, and why?"

"A couple of days ago, I would have told you I would rather

162

be in Chama with Rebecca celebrating Christmas. I would have chosen to be anywhere but here, actually, but I can honestly say that this is the only place I want to be at this moment. This is the best Christmas I've ever had. The love and respect all of you have shown me is unlike anything I've ever experienced—even though a roof caved in on me."

"That's sweet, dear. We feel the same way. Just wish the roof hadn't been part of the equation. How are you feeling?"

Megan rubbed her leg. "My leg is swollen, and it certainly hurts, but I'm fine. It could have been so much worse."

Chapter 23

"We're getting reports that all major thoroughfares will be open tomorrow by 8:00 o'clock in the morning," the D.J. said. "If you're stranded somewhere, sit back, relax, and allow us to provide the soundtrack for your final night of the Christmas season. Next up, we have a little Nat King Cole for you."

"Away in the Manger," filled the room.

"I don't want Christmas to end," Megan said.

"Me either, dear, but it's getting late and we'll need to get you to the hospital in Walsenburg as soon as possible in the morning."

"By the way, I'm going in the ambulance with you," Sarah said.

"And I'll follow you in my car," Brad said.

They hadn't discussed the logistics yet, but Brad wanted to be there for them. Maybe he could accompany them to the hospital, wait until Megan was admitted to the hospital, and then hit the road for Denver to spend a belated holiday with Ryan and Amy. After that was over, he could drive back down to the hospital and hang out there until Megan was released.

"You don't have to do that," Sarah said.

"Yeah, but I want to." Brad filled them in on his plan.

"Now that you have that figured out, don't forget that I'll be handing all of you an index card tomorrow to write down your questions," Ray said. "This is your chance to leave a Nicebreaker legacy."

Everybody chuckled. Brad couldn't help but give his question some serious thought, though, given how important these questions seem to be in the process of getting people to open up about their pain and longings.

Alma made sleeping arrangements for everybody in the living room of the private quarters while Ray fed the wood-burning stove. Sarah tended to Megan's needs, helping her get situated comfortably on the couch and reassuring her that everything was going to be just fine.

* * *

The next morning, Brad was up early to check the weather on the radio. All of the major highways were indeed open. He put his coat and gloves on so he could go take a look at Sarah's car, which was presumably still stranded on the side of the highway near the entrance to the inn. He found Sarah's coat on the coat rack and slipped his hands into the pockets.

"Jackpot." He found the keys.

The snow crunched under his feet and he thought about the events that transpired since he had pulled into the inn just a few days ago. They really had been life-changing. Not only had he found love again, when he didn't even think that was possible, but he felt like he was gaining another daughter. He knew Megan was too old for that, but if she was going to be in

Sarah's life, then she was going to be in his too.

Sarah's car was in worse shape than he imagined. Her passenger side door was caved in, a tire was punctured, and, somehow, the muffler had been ripped off. Initially, she said she had hit a mile-marker sign, but Brad couldn't see one. He got down on his knees, looked under the car, and gasped. A long strip of metal that he couldn't identify was embedded in the underbody. Was it part of the mile-marker sign? *If it had been just a few inches to the right, it would have hit the gas tank and this car would have exploded. It's almost as if she had an angel watching over her.*

* * *

Brad called a towing service for Sarah's car. The nearest shop was in Antonito, which was maybe twenty-five miles away, according to the attendant. Brad re-entered the inn to the aroma of Christmas Delight.

Sarah sat in the kitchen with her hands cupped around a steaming mug. The temperature had definitely dropped inside overnight, but the power was back on, thankfully. Now the furnace just needed time to catch up.

Brad sat down next to Sarah and informed her about her car. "Thank you," she said.

"Glad to do it. So, are we going with the plans we talked about last night?"

They thought about their options for a minute.

"My mom will understand if we postpone Christmas for a bit. I think I'll take Megan's vehicle and follow the ambulance to the hospital. Why don't you just head up to Denver to see your kids, like you had planned? You don't need to stop at the hospital. I'll keep you updated on Megan."

"Okay, that works."

"Megan said her car is set up to accommodate her cerebral palsy, which means the gas and brake are both operated by hand, so she should be able to drive it after she is released. We'll pick up my car in Antonito on the way back, and we'll head to my place from there. I just talked to her and she plans to drive over to Chama to see her friend, Rebecca, for a day or two. That might give us a little time to get to know each other better, if you'd like, before both of our schedules kick into high gear."

"Perfect," he said.

* * *

Alma arranged for an ambulance to transport Megan to the hospital. Everybody showered and packed, except Megan. Sarah packed for her. Ray waived their cabin fees, given their circumstances. Besides, it was never really about the money anyway. He just had to accept lodging fees for the sake of appearance.

"Oh wait," Ray said. "Don't forget that each of you needs to write down your question on an index card." He disappeared into the main area of the lodge for a couple of minutes and returned with new index cards in hand. "Whoa, it is freezing over there. I'm going to have to call my insurance agent today to get the lodge fixed right away." He handed each of them a card.

"I would love to be a fly on the wall next year and hear the answers your residents will provide," Sarah said.

"Me too," Megan said.

They jotted their questions down and everybody took turns embracing. Nobody seemed to want to move. This was always a bittersweet moment for Ray.

The ambulance pulled into the parking lot and two EMTs loaded Megan inside. Sarah climbed behind the wheel of Megan's car and Brad stepped into his vehicle.

"Another Christmas, another group of lives changed," Ray whispered to Alma as the line of vehicles turned right onto Highway 17.

Want to find out what happens to Brad, Sarah, and Megan after they leave Mercy Inn? Order a copy of Comeback, the short story that chronicles their journeys.

If you enjoyed this book, check out The Reunion, Book 2 in "The Mercy Inn" series. Ray and Alma assist a new cast of characters you'll be sure to love.

Other Titles by Lee Warren

In This Series

Mercy Inn: A Christmas Novella (The Mercy Inn Series, Book 1)

Comeback: A Mercy Inn Series Short Story

The Reunion: A Christmas Novella (The Mercy Inn Series, Book 2)

The Revelation: A Christmas Novella (The Mercy Inn Series, Book 3)

Devotionals and Gift Books

Single Servings: 90 Devotions to Feed Your Soul

Fun Facts for Sports Lovers

Inspiring Thoughts for Golfers

Racing for Christ: 50 Devotions for NASCAR Fans

Experiencing Christmas: A 31-Day Family Christmas Devotional

Finishing Well: Living with the End in Mind (A Devotional)

Flying Solo: 30 Devotions to Encourage the Never-Married

Essays

Common Grounds: Contemplations, Confessions, and (Unexpected) Connections from the Coffee Shop

Sacred Grounds: First Loves, First Experiences, and First Favorites

Higher Grounds: When God Steps into the Here and Now

Finding Common Ground: Boxed Set (Books 1-3)

Writing

Write That Devotional Book: From Dream to Reality

Write That Book in 30 Days: Daily Inspirational Readings

You can find out more about Lee Warren's books here:
http://www.leewarren.info/books

Subscribe to Lee's weekly email list (dedicated to slowing down and living deeper), and you'll receive a digital freebie as a thank you. You will also receive notifications about his newest books and become eligible for random giveaways. Sign up here:
http://www.leewarren.info/email-list

Follow Lee on social media:
https://www.facebook.com/leewarrenauthor
https://twitter.com/leewarren

Visit Lee's website:
  http://www.leewarren.info

CPSIA information can be obtained
at www.ICGtesting.com
Printed in the USA
LVHW080010150822
725932LV00001B/140